BOOKS BY KRISTIE COOK

SOUL SAVERS

Recommended Reading Order:

A Demon's Promise

An Angel's Purpose

Genesis: A Soul Savers Novella

Dangerous Devotion

Dark Power

Sacred Wrath

Unholy Torment

Fractured Faith

Age of Angels Part I: Awakened

Age of Angels Part II: Lost

Age of Angels Part III: Marked

Prophecy of the Wolves: (A Soul Savers Tie-In Novella)

Wonder: A Soul Savers Collection of Holiday Short Stories & Recipes

KNIGHTS OF SOULS AND SHADOWS

Knights of Souls and Shadows

HAVENWOOD FALLS

Recommended Reading Order:

Forget You Not

Lose You Not

Break Me Not

The Collector: Awakening

Savage Salvation (Sin & Silk)

Sun & Moon Academy Book One: Fall Semester

Sun & Moon Academy Book Two: Fall Semester

The Winged & the Wicked (with T.V. Hahn)

Havenwood Falls Short Story Anthology 2018

Havenwood Falls Short Story Anthology 2019

Havenwood Falls Short Story Anthology 2020

BOOK OF PHOENIX

The Space Between

The Space Beyond

The Space Within

SOUL SAVERS BOOK 9

AGE
OF
ANGELS

PART II: LOST

KRISTIE COOK

To Stacey & Heather
For reasons

PROLOGUE

*L*ightning flashed across the underbelly of the dark cloud that came out of nowhere, blossoming like black ink against the pale blue of the northern sky. Thunder cracked loudly and rolled throughout the heavens, echoing off the barren landscape. Wind gusted through the gray trees that hadn't seen leaves in years, their tops swaying and creaking as the branches scratched like an old witch's fingertips against the sky.

Like most storms since the War of Armageddon, this one exploded with no warning, whipping up black magic residue and nuclear fallout that still lingered on the Earth's surface since the bombs had been dropped. The chaotic weather wreaked all kinds of havoc across the natural world, forcing what remained of the world's population to remain in their underground bunkers that had been home for the past six-plus years.

Using potent magic, we'd cleared an area around the entrance to our own bunker, nicknamed The Loft, allowing our human residents to enjoy fresh air and real sunlight when the weather allowed. The space now teemed with people hurriedly packing things up and rushing down below. There were no permanent structures yet, but the merchants brought their tables to the surface where they could spread out more compared to the section below where they usually kept shop. Of course, "merchants" and "shops" had a different meaning now—nobody actually sold anything, not for money, anyway. Rather, goods and services were traded for those items beyond the basics that we managed to provide for everyone.

"We" as in Earth's Angels and the rest of the Amadis. The Heavenly Host had deemed this new era on Earth as the Age of Angels and crowned me leader to oversee the rebuilding of civilization. I still had no idea what the hell they were thinking with that decision, but there was too much to do to care anymore. With the help of my council and the rest of our people, we simply went to work. It hadn't been easy. For every two steps forward, we were pushed back three, but hey, we'd at least managed to prevent any more wars from breaking out, even in these desperate times, so there was that.

"I'll take care of the table, Trudy," I hollered over the wind that whipped at my hair, the chestnut locks slapping at my face. I folded her card table as the elderly human woman stuffed knitted goods into a bag, including some of the little dolls she made out of scraps that my girls loved dearly.

"Alexis!" yelled a female voice, my name filled with urgency. I looked over my shoulder to see Teah running toward me. The tall, slender young woman was one of the twins' teachers. I'd seen her cousin Teal, the other teacher, shuffling children inside several minutes ago. "We can't find the girls!"

"Aren't they inside with Teal?"

Teah shook her dark hair, her blue eyes filled with panic. "She took the other children in while I went looking for the twins. I'm so sorry! I don't even know when they might have wandered off."

My gaze swung around the area that had been bustling not too long ago, but was now completely clear, the last of our people making their way through the wide doorway. Surely, they'd just gone inside with everyone else, and the teachers hadn't seen them. My girls had a habit of falling into their own private world, separating themselves from the other kids. All except one.

"What about Charleigh?" I asked.

"She's inside with Teal," Teah shouted.

Then the twins had to be, too. Using my telepathy, I searched for the girls' minds, but I didn't sense them inside. I didn't sense them anywhere outside either. At least, not within our boundaries. Trying not to panic, I made a mental announcement to everyone below, reaching into their minds and ordering them to do a head count and find the twins. One by one, the replies came back: they were nowhere to be seen.

A large, powerful male body suddenly showed up by my side.

"What the hell happened?" Tristan yelled.

Teah's eyes grew wide, her face blanching. My husband could be quite frightening, especially when it came to the safety of our daughters.

"I'm so sorry," is all she managed to say.

"Just get inside," I told her. "We'll find them."

Four of my core council members—and some of our strongest residents—ran out of the entryway to The Loft just as Tristan and I both revealed our wings. With the storm brewing, we didn't have time to do a locator spell.

"Owen and Vanessa, go north," Tristan ordered. "Sheree and Aidan, go east. Alexis and I will take the rest."

Vanessa and Owen immediately took off. While the warlock couldn't quite keep up with her vampire speed, his personal enchantments made him fast enough. Sheree and Aidan both shifted first—Sheree into a tiger and Aidan into a stone beast with wings. I still had a hard time understanding how the gargoyle could fly, as heavy as he was, but he could. They headed east, Sheree on the ground and Aidan not far above her. Tristan and I both took to the sky. He went straight south while I flew west, making wide sweeping arcs to see as much of the terrain below as possible.

Everything was an ugly gray, making it difficult to distinguish objects on the ground. The wind whipped at me as more lightning flashed off toward the north. I could no longer suppress the panic that fought its way from my chest into my throat as minutes passed by with no sighting, no word from the others. We were surrounded by wilderness, the nearest town, Ravenbury, over fifty miles away—if you didn't count the dragon clan by the lake, thirty miles away, and I really didn't want to even think about them. Not when my girls were out here.

This was a dangerous world we lived in. Besides the dragons, demons and zombies frequently roamed the woods outside the magical boundaries that protected The Loft. Gangs of humans occasionally passed through, too, hungry, thirsty, and sometimes driven mad and violent with desperation.

Two six-year-olds could never survive for long out here. Not even my girls, who would eventually be more powerful than everyone, but that was many years in the future.

"*Found them!*" Owen's voice whooped in my head, at the same moment the wind suddenly died and the thunder silenced. I saw my girls' faces through his eyes, and my heart immediately settled, especially when I saw that Sasha, their *lykora*, was with them. The legendary creature would protect them at all costs.

"*This way, Tristan,*" I called out, banking right in the direction of Owen's mind signature—the blip on my mental radar that his mind sent out.

"*You need to see this,*" Vanessa said, her mental voice sounding peculiar.

We found them a few minutes later, over a mile north of The Loft, not far from where that storm had been brewing only moments ago. *How did they get way out here?*

"Momma! Daddy!" Brielle and Elliana squealed, running to us as soon as we dropped to the ground. Closing our wings in and making them vanish, we each scooped one of the girls up into our arms. I squeezed Elliana against me until she grunted. Thank the Angels they were okay. I'd save their reprimand for later.

"Look what we did!" Brielle said from Tristan's arms, gesturing toward Owen and Vanessa—or perhaps toward Sasha who stood behind them, her tail end toward us as she sniffed the air.

"Uncle Owen and Auntie Nessa don't believe us, though." Elliana said with a pout, laying an arm across the back of my neck while giving the other two an accusatory look. Only the twins could get away with calling their vampire aunt such a nickname.

"What is it?" I asked, studying the space just beyond Owen and Vanessa—about a three-foot-wide by four-foot-tall oval shape where the air appeared to . . . swirl. Black vines grew out of the ground, twisting and turning to create a frame around the anomaly. My head tilted. "And what the hell is wrong with Sasha?"

The *lykora*, no longer hidden behind her usual glamour of a small white dog, sported her true appearance—large and wild like a winged wolf, her tail bushed out and standing on end, the fur along her backbone bristling, and black tiger stripes darkening against the white and gray fur. A low growl rumbled in her throat, her lip curling when the tremor reached her muzzle in a vicious snarl. The hairs on my arms rose to match hers, a reaction not only to her but to the shift in energy as I took a step closer.

"A portal?" Tristan asked, his smooth voice laced with concern and suspicion.

"Yes, but not one of mine," Owen answered, scrubbing his hand through his straw-colored hair. The powerful warlock was trained by a sorceress, and one of the few in the world who could create portals, allowing for easier transportation, especially considering there were no longer airplanes or even cars. "And it doesn't feel like any of the others, either."

We didn't know who else had been making them, but we did know Owen wasn't the only one who could. Even before the bombs dropped, we'd found random portals hanging in the air, leading to all sorts of places throughout the world, sometimes nearby and sometimes maddeningly oceans away. We'd once been caught up in a loop where the portal kept depositing us back in the place we'd just tried to leave.

Studying this one, I nodded. "Something's definitely not right about it. It feels . . ." I shuddered at the eerie feeling spidering down my spine. "*Dark.*"

Tristan moved closer to me, his arm muscles tensing around Brielle. "I feel it, too."

"Exactly," Owen said.

"It's okay, Momma," Elli assured. "Our friends are there."

Brie nodded her head enthusiastically. "That's why we made it. They want to come visit us."

Tristan and I exchanged a sideways glance before looking at Owen and Vanessa expectantly.

"*They must have found it when they ran off,*" Vanessa explained.

"We didn't find it!" Elli argued, catching us by surprise. I didn't think my mind had been open to her. "We *made* it! Brie and me, all by ourselves." She puffed out her chest and lifted her chin defiantly.

"We'll talk about that later," I said to her before returning my attention to Owen and Vanessa. "Do you know where it goes?"

Vanessa shook her white-blonde head.

"We weren't about to check it out with the twins," Owen said. "But watch."

As he stepped forward to approach the portal, the vines surrounding it grew and twisted, long thorns sprouting along the branches and needle-sharp points lashing out at him.

"You don't want to go there," Brielle whispered.

"It's for our friends to come here," Elliana added quietly.

My skin prickled with their words and the premonitory tone as a sense of dread and death pulsed from the portal.

Tristan and I looked at each other for a long moment, a wordless conversation passing through us. Daemoni? Demons? It felt more Otherworldly than even Hell, but whatever was on the other side needed to fucking stay there. Tristan gave a curt nod in agreement.

"Shut that thing down," I ordered Owen. "*Now*."

The warlock's hands moved in front of him, building his power, and then thrust out toward the portal, casting a spell. Nothing happened. He tried again, harder this time.

"That's not working," I gritted through a clenched jaw as that dark energy intensified, growing and feeling like it raced toward us and would burst through at any moment, as though it knew we were trying to shut it out.

"I'm *trying*," Owen grunted as he cast another spell. The shimmering air finally stopped swirling. He cast again, but nothing else happened. The dark energy no longer pulsed off the thing, though. As we waited for several minutes, the air in the portal seemed to solidify, looking like thick, translucent glass.

"Seal it, shield it, and cloak it," I said. "We don't need anyone finding this. We'll check back on it tomorrow."

Sometimes the portals simply disappeared. Maybe this one would, too.

If not? If some dark entity wanted to challenge us? Well, we'd annihilate it just as we had before. This was the Age of Angels. It was our time to rule.

CHAPTER 1

10 YEARS LATER

*W*ings the colors of amethyst and obsidian spread out wide to each side of me, carving through the air like a blade through water. They carry me toward home—toward safety and comfort, love and family, everything that's the opposite of what's out here in the wild. Especially today. I can't quite pinpoint why, though. Nothing remarkable has happened, and we've had many dark days since the war, but something about the air today feels unusually dreary and . . . thick. Heavy. As though an ominous energy weaves through the air currents, a sense of foreboding trailing over my wings and skating along my spine like phantom fingertips.

Home. The thought keeps me going, the promise of a good meal, time with my daughters, and strong arms to hold me a beacon of light in the gloom of this day.

The flatlands of what had once been the great central plains of the United States pass below me in a blur of muted color, mostly dull grays and browns in swirls of gradation that make the earth's surface appear as though it's been tie-dyed. Of course, the truth of what causes the surreal-looking landscape isn't fun or pretty. Nuclear and black magic bombs destroyed the world nearly seventeen years ago, followed by Angel blood that has ever so slowly begun to renew life—life that's dormant now due to winter maintaining its icy grip, although we'd just celebrated the summer solstice.

I want to blame the weather for today's unusual sense of pending doom. After all, clouds block the sun, making the sky colorless, and darker ones roll in from the west, promising yet another blizzard. Powerful gusts of wind have picked up in the last few minutes, heaving against my large wings and rocking me in the air; more than once I'm reminded of when I'd first sprouted these appendages and winds like this had sent me careening into a pile of boulders. They are now a natural part of me, feeling like I've always had them, no different than my arms and legs. The wind is cold against my face yet refreshing because it somehow feels lighter, and I smell and taste snow on the air.

I ponder what color it will be this time—pink or green would definitely bring some needed cheer, and hopefully it won't be the ugly brown of the last storm. Except for the first couple of years, when it was a dingy gray, snow of just about every color has fallen in the winters since the war. Not even our scientifically brightest have figured out exactly what causes the colored snow. Probably because science has very little to do with it. Magic permeates our world now. Which is also the reason that a blizzard seems imminent in late June, summer yet to come to this part of the world that would normally be sweltering by now.

As I soar about fifty feet above the ground, a small team from The Loft travels on foot over what had once been luscious fields of wheat and corn. I am their eyes in the sky and the voice in their minds, telepathically alerting them to any troubles ahead, whether it's the cliff side of a canyon carved into the earth, or a group of Demons or horde of zombies to eliminate.

Before the war, I might have laughed at the idea of zombies being real. I'd accepted vampires, shifters, and mages, but zombies? No way. But my asinine sperm-donor Lucas created them when he started the war, mixing black magic with science, resulting in some kind of necromancy virus. His goal had been to give all the Demons coming from Hell bodies to possess, but they have little interest in reanimated corpses. They want fresh humans whose souls they can devour. Whether Lucas had intended it or not, the zombie virus spread exponentially, making all humans carriers. So when they die, there's a good chance they'll come back, mindless and with a craving for flesh that rivals a newborn vampire's thirst for blood.

So engrossed in the thought of getting home with my family before this new storm hits, I nearly forget our purpose for this run. For any run, because supply trips are never only about the supplies. Every time we're out, we have multiple objectives to serve—search for people and help them find shelter and safety, preferably within an established community; take only the bare minimal resources we need for our people and transfer the rest to the community with the greatest need of the moment; scavenge for special requests from our own people at The Loft, as well as the people in the communities we serve; deal with any of the gangs that dare to challenge us; permanently kill the zombies and clear out the Demons.

That part of our post-Armageddon life hasn't changed over the years. More and more responsibilities have piled on us since the world emerged from their bunkers, and civilization has tried—and often failed—to rebuild.

It's been over sixteen years since Lucas and the Ancients, creators of the Daemoni, opened a gate to Hell to bring Satan to our physical world. Well, first, Lucas effectively killed the majority of life on Earth with the dirty bombs, left a bunch of zombies instead, and opened rifts in the veil that separated the physical realm from the Otherworld. He essentially brought Hell to Earth, and Demons came in droves. When we were able to close the gate before Satan could rise, most of the Demons were sucked back in.

Or so we thought.

As an Earth Angel, I'd been warned by Heaven's Angels that some Demons remained after the war, but their idea of "some" and mine are apparently quite different. We've been working on eradicating them ever since, killing tens of thousands, yet we seem to make no headway. In fact, sometimes I feel as though they're like the zombies—for each one we dispatch, five more show up. They seem to be everywhere.

So when I almost miss the one right below me, that says a lot about how eager I am to return home to my family. The smell hits me first—not the stink of rotten flesh like the zombies, but the putrid odor of sulfur and brimstone. Then I see it.

Oranges and yellows make up this one's mottled skin. Four horns adorn its head, which we've learned over the years indicates its power—the more horns, the more powerful and harder to dispatch (technically, a Demon can't be killed; it can only be sent back to Hell). Four horns mean fairly strong. The most any of us have seen so far is seven. This creature's leathery wings are closed tight to its back as it travels on cloven hooves over the ground—for now. Its whip-like tail with several barbs at the end trails behind it, cutting a swath into the gray snow and dirt.

I consider watching the Demon and alerting my traveling party who are about a half-mile behind me of its presence. They often like to make a game out of hunting and killing with ongoing competitions for number of kills. If we actually counted, Tristan and I would top the list by far. Ragan and her partner Ryder, both supernatural hunters and human, top the list instead, pretty dead even, though with hundreds of kills fewer than Tristan or me. And he and I don't even do these runs very often.

The Demons just seem to be attracted to us like magnets when they sense our presence. Fools.

Although I'm hidden behind a magic cloak and shield that make me invisible to most, the Demon seems to look right up at me, and its nostrils flare. When its wings spread wide like huge black sails behind its back, I know there's no point to wait for the group on the ground to catch up. If I don't act now, the beast will make this a fight in the air anyway. Sometimes, I'd be up for the sparring match before taking it out. Sometimes, the rush of adrenaline is welcome after all the mundane activities of managing The Loft and trying to keep the rest of the world in check. Such a fight feeds the warrior in me who sees hardly any action anymore.

But right now, I just want to go home. My inner warrior will have to be happy with the quick kill that will return this Demon to Hell to never bother another human soul again. Well, that's the theory anyway. I've been questioning that theory.

I nosedive for the ground before the creature even has a chance to launch at me. Two swords are strapped to my back, but I have no need of them. My favorite dagger's already in my hand, my arm extended in front of me, blade aimed at the beast's throat. With a swoop and a swipe of my blade, the horned head rolls off the neck and drops like a stone to its feet, where the brown snow melts from its black blood and the gray dirt underneath darkens.

Huh. I expected more of a fight, but it never even knew how close I'd come before I ended its time here in this world. The head's lips curl upward as the Demon lets out a growl before disappearing with a poof of sulfur that makes my eyes water and my stomach lurch. I soar up high to resume my flight home, at least another hour to the east.

But the wail below me stops me dead.

My breath catches at the despairing sound. Not a Demon or a zombie, but someone of this world, probably a normal human. Someone in a great deal of pain.

I spin, ready to fly to it and help, but again stop dead. My heart plummets to hell at the sight below me. A woman's figure, on her knees, her breath puffing out in white clouds as she screams and sobs over a prone male body. Blood gushes into the dead ground at the top of the body, where the head should be. *Should* being the key factor here. Because the head is not attached to the body but lay several feet away.

And they are right where I'd just offed that Demon.

My lungs seize up, trapping the air in my chest, and my heart lodges itself in my throat. They hadn't been there thirty seconds ago! Where did they come from? I hadn't sensed their mind signatures or anything! What happened to him?

A terrible, *horrifying* thought occurs to me. *No.* I shake my head violently, denying the possibility. *It can't be.* I sink to the ground as I breathlessly stare at the wailing woman who beats her fists on the dead man's chest.

"Steve! No, please, you can't leave me!" she scream-sobs, as though she could convince him to reattach his head and return to this life. Her dirty hair is matted to her head, no hat covering it or gloves on her hands. Both of their jackets are thin and threadbare, their pants torn and ragged. They appear to have been living in the wild for quite some time. How have they made it alone this long, especially through the endless winter? Maybe they aren't alone . . .

I don't know what to do. I want to console her. I want to hug her and give her a shoulder to cry on. I want to provide her comfort, take her to her people, if she has any, or to our people who can give her food, running water for a shower, clean clothes, and a bed.

But the truth is sinking in. A heavy, hot stone in the pit of my stomach.

I did this.

"*Alexis, where are you?*" Vanessa's voice sounds distant in my mind at first, barely audible because my brain is a little distracted at the moment. Of my team, she's the closest, of course—the vampire runs almost as fast as I fly.

No, I think again.

"*No what?*" Vanessa asks.

11

I . . . I don't know what I've done.

"Tell me where you are. We can't find you."

I glance around at my surroundings and telepathically share the view with her and the others, blurry as it is because tears fill my eyes. I purposely avoid showing them the woman and the corpse. They'll see the gory scene soon enough—like now as Vanessa crests the bluff in a streak of black leather and white hair. She nearly falls over, she stops so fast, and her mouth parts as she takes in the woman, the corpse, the head. She lifts her white-blonde head as ice-blue eyes sweep the area for me, although she can't see me. Owen keeps a cloak on me at all times to protect me from crack-jobs who shoot at anything they see in the sky. We lost several of our bird-shifters in the early years because of them. Bullets aren't a lethal threat to me, but they can be quite the inconvenience.

To your left, I say, and Vanessa lifts her chin in acknowledgement.

"Help me," the woman cries when she sees she's no longer alone.

"What happened?" Vanessa asks as she slowly approaches them. There isn't really much she can do to help. The damage is quite permanent.

The woman sucks in a snotty, snuffly breath then shrugs and shakes her head. "I . . . I don't know. He was only a little ahead of me. He's always a little ahead of me, trying to protect me. As soon as I came through that hedge line, I found him like this. I'd just seen him seconds before! How—how—"

Her own fresh sobs cut her off. She leans over, drops her head to Steve's unmoving chest, and cries. I can't fathom how she isn't gagging. The sickening odor of sulfur hangs heavily in the air. At least . . . I think it does. I'm so confused. I don't know anymore.

"What happened?" This time Vanessa addresses me. I know because my half-sister's question is silent, in my mind.

I finally manage a few shallow breaths. *I killed . . . a Demon. At least . . . . I thought . . . I don't know, Vanessa. I don't fucking know!*

Panic threatens to consume me. How could I mistake a Demon for a human? Unless . . .

"Was the man possessed?" Vanessa asks, but I hear the doubt in her mental voice. Possessed humans don't look like Demons—they look like humans. In fact, only supernaturals and hunters can even detect the Demon inside, by the dark energy and sometimes a faint smell of sulfur that's undetectable to Norman senses.

I only saw a Demon, I say at the same moment the rest of our party, all slower than the vampire, run onto the scene.

"Ugh!" Owen's cheeks puff and his Adam's apple bobs as he gags.

"Told you I smelled sulfur," Sheree says. She's in her human form, thank the Angels, because this woman doesn't need to be further freaked out by a rampant tiger. Although humans are well aware that they share their world with the supernatural, not all appreciate it. In fact, many, if not most, prefer to have nothing to do with us, all based in fear. So yeah, Sheree in her animal form wouldn't have been a good idea. Her eyes are yellow, though, and the pupils elongated. I catch her claws retracting into her fingers as she takes in the crying woman. She rushes to the human's side and provides the comfort that Vanessa doesn't know how to give and I'm in no shape to.

"*Alexis?*" Owen telepathically searches for me.

By the elm tree.

He looks over in my direction, but not even he can see through his own cloaks. He can't see me still staring at the dead man, my arms hugging my chest, my hand at my throat, tears rolling down my cheeks.

What have I done?

"*Smells like you killed a Demon,*" Owen says.

I nod, though nobody can see the gesture. *That's what I thought, too, but . . .*

"*But what? There's no mistaking that odor.*"

I think I killed this man, too.

There's no reply at first, but I feel the shock that strikes through everyone's mind signatures—what I call the strings of energy I pick up in my head that represent a thinking mind. Everyone's is unique, like their thumb print or signature. Only I can sense them, even when I open my mind to others' for telepathic conversations like this.

"*Then he wasn't a man,*" Sheree finally replies while consoling the grieving woman.

My teeth set on edge. *He very obviously was! I mean, he wasn't . . . Shit! I don't know!*

"*He had to have been possessed,*" Vanessa says, more convincingly than before.

But I saw a Demon! I insist. *Yellow and orange with four horns, barbed tail, hooves, and all. It wasn't a man! But . . .*

My stomach clenches, threatening to heave, and my entire body trembles. The sight before me proves otherwise. I hadn't dispatched a

Demon. I'd killed a Norm—a normal human—who means something to this woman and maybe to others, as well. I have no idea how I could have been so mistaken. But I obviously had been.

I squeeze my eyes shut, wishing this is a bad dream and I'll wake from it when I open my eyes again. I see the Demon behind my eyelids, just as it had been only minutes ago. In my mind's eye, I pull back my perspective, as though flying backward, up into the air, reversing the events and taking in the surrounding area. Maybe the body doesn't lie in the exact same spot as where I'd killed the Demon. The landscape is pretty monotonous, so perhaps I'm simply confused. A light gray, almost white boulder, much lighter than the dirty snow around it, juts out of the earth near the Demon, one side of it narrowed, almost like an arrow pointing at the beast two yards away.

I open my eyes. Vanessa's perched on the same boulder. One side of it points at the corpse and the woman about two yards away.

Sheree's voice drones in the background of my pulse pounding in my ears. She asks the woman questions about where they'd been going, where they'd come from, if they'd run into any gangs, zombies, or any other problems. I skim the woman's mind, and while she tells Sheree about the gang they'd narrowly avoided a couple of weeks ago, I see the events play out in her mind.

"What about Steve? Had he been acting any differently lately?"

The woman looks up at Sheree and blinks away tears. She doesn't have to voice her answer for me to know. I see it in her thoughts. Steve had most certainly been acting weird lately. Grumpier, almost mean. She'd chalked it up to their being hangry. They haven't eaten anything substantial for weeks, only the little bit they've been able to scavenge from abandoned homes and towns, which means hardly enough to survive on. One has to be clever and persistent to find anything good left anymore—everywhere has already been looted several times over.

The woman swallows and whispers, "How did you know?"

"Shit." Vanessa swears under her breath, too quietly for the woman to hear. She looks over in my direction. "*See? Possessed.*"

And that's supposed to make me feel better? I ask. *It doesn't make Steve any less dead.*

"*But not at your hand. He was already dead.*"

How do we know?

"*My guess would be because all you saw was Demon, not any hint of*

14

man," Owen says. "*All you sensed was evil. Right?*"

I pull in a ragged breath. *Of course.*

I'm not as sure as I make myself sound, though. Because I can't remember. I saw a Demon. I did what I do: I killed it. Sent it back to Hell, anyway. I didn't even think about sensing for anything other than evil.

But . . . surely I would have automatically sensed something else. Right? Knowing the difference, sensing the subtleties, is a part of me. Part of who and what I am. A trace of any hope for the man's soul would have stopped me. Right?

I can only hope because I no longer know.

Bent over Steve, the woman's body starts trembling, and at first, I think she's sobbing again, but then it becomes clear: she's laughing. A giggle escalates into a strange, high-pitched cackle, then she throws her head back and howls. Pitch black bleeds into her eyes with a red glow behind them.

"Thank. You." She gasps the words between guffaws. "He was getting on my nerves. Some people just can't handle being us."

Then she's gone. Just gone. She's disappeared with a poof of sulfur, leaving my team to stand there with their mouths hanging open.

"What the hell just happened?" Vanessa demands before taking off at vampire speed, probably to search for the woman. The Demon.

Sheree stares at her hands as if she's never seen them before. "I touched her. I felt nothing. Smelled nothing. How . . . how did we not know? At *all?*"

"Seems the Demons are getting better at hiding from us," Owen mutters.

I consider this all the way home, lost in thought and silence as is everyone else. I can't make sense of it. Yes, the Demon in the woman hid itself well from us and easily vanished. Vanessa searched a ten-mile radius but found no sign of her. But the one in the man—I'd seen it clear as day. In fact, it had been the *human* that had been hidden from me. Did he do that on purpose? Or did she orchestrate the whole thing? Are the Demons not only getting better at hiding from us but growing smarter? Evolving? I balk at the thought. This is the last thing our world needs.

All I know for certain is what I'd thought would be a quick Demon extermination on the way home to my family turns out to have completely shifted my world.

CHAPTER 2

*a*s I approach The Loft, there's no sign of its existence. A few hundred acres of woods surrounds the enormous underground bunker except for a snow-dusted gravel road that leads up to the main entrance at the bottom of a hill. A garage door cut into the side of the hill is the only sign that there *might* be life around—or had been in the Before time. At least, that's what any outsiders see because Owen and the other mages have it heavily warded, shielded, cloaked, and muffled. If you aren't a resident and included in the wards, you'll subconsciously avoid the area, skirting the perimeter. If you happen to know we're there, you still can't get in without an invite and clearance. But once you do enter, you step into the beginnings of a small town burgeoning outside the overhead door in the hill.

In the past couple of years, we've cleared out about twenty acres, using the wood to build a few permanent structures. Although, "permanent" is relative these days. They aren't our first attempts because the shields aren't impervious to the weather and what comes with it—the electrical storms and untimely blizzards whip up black magic and sometimes even nuclear fallout from those parts hardest hit, scattering residue across the Earth's surface. So cleared areas that had been deemed safe don't stay that way. We've lost several buildings over the years—including a cabin my family lived in for a while, up until a year ago—to a variety of (un)natural disasters, including acid rain, tornadoes, and earthquakes. The mages are constantly trying to improve their techniques to fortify the structures, but if we've learned anything since the war, it's that nothing lasts forever.

This is why civilization around the world hasn't advanced further. The dystopian stories written before the war never included black magic within the mix of rebuilding. It's changed everything. And rather than improving over time, it often seems like it's only growing worse.

So we only use the buildings when the weather allows to stable our animals and to provide a bigger space for a few occupations, like blacksmithing and woodworking. The merchants set up tents and tables outside, where people trade tokens they've earned for little extras beyond what everyone receives—food, shelter, and clothing. As for shelter and security, we still have everything we need below in The Loft. Our little area on the surface serves the primary purpose of giving us a respite from life underground.

I arrive several minutes ahead of the others, and when I pass through the shield, I find that everything has been packed up and tucked away safely below for the pending storm, including the livestock. I walk up to the overhead door, where the words AK's Angels, an image of wings, and lots of swirly lines decorate the paint job around the garage door. I touch a pattern into the swirly symbols, and the door begins to open. I inhale deeply.

Home sweet home.

While striding down the long tunnel, I try to shake the thoughts that have been swirling through my mind about the Demons. Time to switch my hat from warrior and leader to mom and wife. Easier said than done, though, when the image of the headless man keeps replaying in my mind. Whether it was real or a mirage doesn't matter—I still feel that sense of dread in the pit of my stomach. As I pass my office and the conference room, I pause and consider calling a council meeting to discuss what happened. I nix the idea quickly, though, and continue down the path toward the bustling center of The Loft.

The mouth-watering scents wafting from the kitchen remind me it's almost dinnertime, not an ideal time to be holding a meeting. When I pass the large dining area with its mishmash of tables and chairs and see the first wave of Loft residents lined up at the buffets, I realize it's even later than I thought. I've learned the hard way that nothing ever gets done when my council is hungry.

Besides, I need time to process, maybe discuss it with Tristan. No, not maybe. Definitely.

The dining area sits at the center of The Loft's vast space that had once been a limestone mine before it became a survival prepper's paradise—and then became a real-life bunker when the bombs dropped. The original owner, Brogan, had already established the basics in the largest section, where limestone columns support the high ceilings that are more than tall enough to have allowed trucks to pass through back when the mine was operating. He built a training area complete with a shooting range, kitchen, dining room, a medical ward, and residences—enough space and stocked supplies for over a thousand people to survive for several years. And he hadn't even developed the entire area that had been cleared out by the miners. We have since then, expanding the outer areas for underground crops and livestock.

Water's pumped in and air's recycled, and we have electricity, but lightbulbs have become harder and harder to find, so candles, fire sconces, and magical orbs provide most of the lighting, dim as it is. Some of the residents have added homey touches and created beautiful landscapes on the limestone walls to make it all feel a little cheerier—and not so confining.

Past the bustling center sprawls the residential area, rows and rows of narrow, two-story structures containing one- and two-room apartments. Everyone on my core council lives on the same block, a few rows back from the dining area. Not too far away when we're needed, but not smack in the middle of the noise, either.

I remove the strap that holds my swords to my back, the sheathe for my dagger on my right hip, and the belt that keeps my knife in place on my left thigh as I climb the metal steps to our family apartment. Although we lead The Loft (and beyond) and many even consider us royalty, we've never taken more than anyone else is allotted. We'd started with one room like all singles, couples, and three-person families do. As the twins grew, though, we realized we really did need a second room. So we took over where Sheree had lived next door when she moved in with Aidan. It worked out for all of us. The cabin up top had been a nice change for as long as it lasted, but our space down here is . . . home.

As I walk in and toss my weapons onto a shelf in our living room-slash-bedroom, I find Tristan sitting in the armchair, reviewing some kind of architectural plans. He takes one look at my face, stands, and opens his large, powerful arms. I walk right into them and bury my face in his chest as those wonderful arms wrap me in their comfort. Still after all these years, his intoxicating scent and touch calm me, bringing a sense of peace that I desperately need at the moment. When I'm in his arms, I feel like everything is right in the world.

Until the noise on the other side of the thin wall reminds me that it isn't.

"Do I even want to know?" I grumble against Tristan's chest.

His muscles vibrate as he chuckles. "They've been at it all day. I don't know what's gotten into them, but they're definitely in a mood."

"They're teenagers. That's all we need to know." I sigh and pull back, tilting my head to look up at my husband's beautiful face. His hazel gaze holds mine, the emerald green around the outside of the irises mesmerizing me for a moment.

Then the door connecting our room to the twins' bangs open.

"It's about time," Brielle snaps as she charges into our room, strands of her coppery hair, nearly the same color as mine, flying wildly out of her braid. Unlike her twin, she doesn't care as much about her appearance, the one thing that makes it easy for others to tell them apart. "Can we go eat now? I'm starving." Her mahogany eyes blaze with a heated energy that's more common for her twin. Brielle is usually our calm one. She's definitely in a mood.

"For real," Elliana agrees, stomping in after her sister and crossing her arms over her chest. "Maybe if Brie has something in her mouth, she'll finally shut the hell up."

Tristan and I glance at each other. It's unusual for them to fight so vehemently with each other. Usually, they prefer to gang up on me.

"Hey, Mom, we're so glad you're back," I say, mocking their voices. "We really missed you and can't wait to have dinner with you and discuss our days."

They both stare at me as though I've grown a second head.

I sigh and turn toward the door, silently mumbling about teenagers. "Fine. Let's go eat."

We head back toward the dining area, where many residents are already seated, waving or nodding as we pass them by, then returning to their conversations over their meals. We join the end of the line, but I leave Tristan and the girls to pop my head into the kitchen to check on Blossom.

"How's it going?" I ask my best friend as she piles rolls into a basket to take out to the buffet.

She grins when she sees me, a salve to my heart, and lets go of one of her typical word-vomits about what the kitchen's serving tonight. While everyone else had been battening down the hatches for the blizzard, the kitchen had been making a hearty stew and baking bread for dinner. When she isn't sitting in on council meetings and occasionally going along on a mission, Blossom manages all the food resources for The Loft, overseeing the cooks. She's mostly known for her cakes, though.

"Did you know Owen and Vanessa got their hands on cocoa beans the other day?" she asks as she nudges me with her elbow. "You know what that means."

My spirit soars. "Yes! Chocolate. You have no idea how badly I need it."

She laughs. "I think the girls do, too. Charleigh's mood is all over the place."

We commiserate over raising teenaged girls, as we tend to do often. Charleigh came into Blossom and Jax's life when the twins were still babies. So close in age, the three of them have been practically inseparable since.

"Your chocolate cake is a cure-all," I say before pushing through the double-doors, returning to my family who's nearly at the front of the line.

Thirty minutes later, I eye my slice of chocolatey goodness, my mouth watering for it. Unfortunately, the twins' moods have not improved. They're usually much more agreeable, but they've apparently chosen tonight to be full-on teenagers, angst and everything.

"This place is so boring," Elli complains as she picks at her dinner. So much for them being starving. "I'm tired of it. Why can't we move to Misery's Edge?"

"This is our home," I say. "At least until Amadis Island is rebuilt."

"Oh, great," Elli snarks. "So we get to go from underground to an island. Like that will be better." I can practically hear her eyes roll in her head.

"Misery's Edge is a norm city," Tristan points out. "You know they don't like us there."

"You mean it *was*," Brielle says. "It's not really much of a city anymore, since the big tornado and then the earthquake. That's what I've heard, anyway." At least her tone and mood has improved with food, if not her sister's.

"Which is why we're back to being underground," I remind Elliana.

That same tornado had been the last event to wipe out our little settlement on the surface, when it blew away everything about a year ago. We lost three lives that day. Considering the weather has only grown stranger and less predictable since then—like this never-ending winter—and that The Loft has served us well for as long as it has, nobody's been in a hurry to rebuild again.

The twister tore its way across nearly two hundred miles of land, eventually slamming into Misery's Edge. The flourishing town had started as a marketplace a little south of where St. Louis had once been. The highways of the Before time were unusable—either destroyed or blocked by burnt-out cars and trucks—and big cities were avoided because they were the hardest hit by both the bombs and the zombies. When people emerged and set out to seek life outside their bunkers, they often stopped to rest and to barter for goods and services at this location, where several trails came to a crossroads on the banks of the Mississippi River. Many moved on, but not all. Some settled, and it's grown from there. Well, it had been growing, becoming the closest thing to a city until the double-whammy of the tornado followed shortly after by an earthquake.

"I'm sure Misery's Edge has rebuilt some, at least," Elli says.

"And I'm sure it's still a human city," I reply.

There has been a lot of understandable prejudice against the supernatural, especially in the beginning. After all, it'd been the Daemoni's vampires, shifters, and mages that started everything with attacks on the humans before the bombs had dropped. It took the Amadis a long time to convince humans that not all supernaturals are evil or even a threat, especially when they'd been misled to believe that I had been the reason for the war. The Loft isn't the only mixed community, though, and the others have served as proof that we can help humanity. Still, some places just don't want supernaturals around, whether because they think we have an unfair advantage or because they want humans to feel like they have a safe, *normal* place of their own.

Misery's Edge is of both mindsets. The town's mayor, who goes by the single name of Ranker, despises supernaturals and especially us, after we'd run him off from Ravenbury, another town he'd tried to seize control of years ago. He never misses an opportunity to make his hate clear.

"Why don't you do something about that?" Elliana gripes. "Isn't that prejudice? You're always talking about how we should be loving and accepting of everyone. Shouldn't they?"

"I have no control over them," I say.

"We don't interfere with their laws," Tristan adds.

She snorts. "I would, if I were in charge. Nobody would be able to tell me what to do."

"Thank the Angels you aren't in charge," Brie mutters, and I can't agree more.

Elli makes a face at her twin, then leans forward on the table. "Weren't you bitching earlier today that you were bored, too? That you're tired of the people here?"

"That's not what I said!" Brie protests.

"Oh, yeah." Elli nods. "You're right. You were complaining about how there are no *boys* here."

Brie's face flushes. "I . . . You . . . you suck, Elliana!"

I look at Tristan, who's running his hand through his hair, looking like he wishes he were anywhere but here. I recall a time when I'd walked in on him with ribbons in his hair and paint on his nails after an afternoon of Daddy time with the girls. He's always willing to do anything to put smiles on his daughters' faces, but that's become harder and harder to do over the years. He loves them to death, but he struggles with parenting teenaged girls. Sometimes it seems the only way he knows how to relate with them, especially with Elli, is when they're training. Like right now, I know he wishes he could take them to the sparring ring and work them until they're too exhausted to even think about anything but sleep.

"What about the new family?" I ask, trying to diffuse the situation before the girls really lit into each other. They normally got along like best friends rather than sisters, but when they do argue, it's almost as bad as real war. "Don't they have kids your age? Those are some new faces."

"Just one," Elli says like I'm stupid, her tone *this close* to getting her in trouble. I raise a brow at her. "He's a boy," she adds, as though it explains everything.

"Who likes other boys," Brielle finishes. "So no, Mom, not exactly our type."

"Like you even have a type," Elli says. "You wouldn't know what to do if a boy dropped his pants and came onto you anyway."

Tristan stands so fast, his chair falls over. I hope only I can hear the growl in his chest. "And I'm done here. Are you girls finished with your dinner?"

"Yeah, this tastes like crap anyway," Elli says, pushing her bowl away.

"Elliana Katerina," I say between gritted teeth, done with her attitude. "Be grateful you have anything to eat!"

"Ugh. Don't go momming me now. And sorry, but I'm tired of the same old thing practically every night."

I consider telling her about the malnourished woman I saw just today, but then remember that had been no woman, and that sickening feeling returns. So instead, I gesture at my plate of chocolate cake, which makes me feel a little better. "It's not the same old thing, but if you don't finish your dinner, you don't get any dessert."

She eyes my cake with longing, but then looks at her bowl of half-finished stew. Pulling a face, she stands. "It's not worth it. I'll puke if I eat another bite of that."

"Same," Brielle agrees, also standing.

"I thought you were starving," I say.

She shrugs. "Not for this."

"I think you two need some training with your dad," Tristan says before I can "mom" them again. I laugh internally—yep, I don't always have to read his mind to know what he's thinking.

"Da-ad," Elli whines, "we already trained all day."

"Obviously not enough, if you have all this angry energy," he replies.

"It's not that. We're just . . ." Brielle glances at her dad, before stepping closer to me and dropping her voice. As if he can't hear her anyway. "It's that time of the month for us."

Ah. Well, that explains a lot.

I can tell he tries to suppress it, but Tristan cringes. "Yeah, I'm definitely out of here."

Charleigh bounces up to us as Tristan strides off, her orange hair shiny under the lights. "You two finally done eating? Let's go. Mom saved us some cake."

She jerks her head toward the kitchen. The girls gather their dishes, about to follow.

"Hey." I drop my hands to my hips.

"Sorry, Mom," Brielle says. "We just need some girl time. I'm sure you have a ton of work to do anyway."

23

As if they don't get plenty of girl time. They stride off without waiting for a reply. I always have work to do, but tonight is supposed to be about them.

"Actually," I call out after them, and they turn around expectantly. "I'm done for the night."

No sooner do the words tumble out of my mouth than the guards up at the door call for me.

"*Alexis, we got something going on up here,*" Ragan says when I open my mind to her. "*Looks like James got himself into a shitload of trouble.*"

CHAPTER 3

*G*reat. I'm not surprised, though. The supernatural hunter James is an ass and a magnet for trouble. *Do you need me up there? We have teen girl drama going on down here.*

"*Yeah, sorry, but we've got one pissed off dragon up here.*"

Shit. Fine you win—but just barely. I stand while relaying the information to Tristan.

"Never mind," I say to the girls. "You go on. Let Blossom know if you need more . . . you know."

Thank the Angels for Blossom and her creative magic—she'd found a way to replicate feminine hygiene products since there are no manufacturing plants anymore. There have been numerous skirmishes over resources throughout the years, but that might have been the first time another world war had nearly broken out—when women ran out of pads and tampons.

Brielle's face turns a bright pink, and Elliana rolls her eyes. Then they turn away and hurry off before I can embarrass them any further. Not that anyone is paying attention at the moment, but they'd be sixteen years old in a couple of months. I remember that it seems like everyone is watching you at that age, looking for some reason to humiliate you. That self-consciousness hasn't changed with the times. Especially for them—they've been at the center of attention since they were born.

With a sigh, I grab my plate of chocolate cake, not about to miss out, and head up to The Loft's main entrance. Tristan meets me at the junction to the tunnel that leads upward. When we duck under the overhead door and step outside, we find Ragan with her arms crossed and her boot tapping as she stares at James, a crumpled and charred motorcycle, and a very pissed off dragon. He hasn't even bothered to shift into his human form, which I take as a bad sign. I admire the beautiful beast, though, with blue and teal scales, a body bigger than a semi-truck, and a wingspan of at least fifty feet. Smoke curls out from his nostrils. *Yep, he's mad.*

"What's going on?" I ask.

The dragon's deep voice booms in my head. "*Your hunter attacked one of mine.*"

"James," I gasp, "you *attacked* them?"

I can't believe I'm asking this. We've been able to maintain some kind of peace with the dragon clan that lives by the lake that The Loft uses as our water source. Aidan the gargoyle claims this is practically a miracle. Dragons aren't known to get along with anyone, especially for this long. They do feel some appreciation toward Tristan and me, though, because our actions led to their freedom from Hell during the war. Satan had captured them centuries ago and kept them hostage in the Otherworld.

Or maybe the Netherworld? I've never understood that world that isn't ours.

Sometimes I wonder if Aidan is right and freeing the dragons had been a mistake. There are a few other dragon clans around the world who haven't been quite as tolerant as these, causing all kinds of problems. Tristan and I have managed to avoid similar issues with the local clan, but then James returned, and he just can't seem to leave them alone.

It was probably a mistake to let him back into The Loft. He'd been gone for years, but apparently he'd pissed off all the hunter groups he'd found and ended up at our doorstep, begging for forgiveness. If he'd had a tail, it would have been between his legs. Ragan pleaded with me not to let him back in, but I couldn't bring myself to turn him away. He's here on probation, though, which he might have just ruined.

"I was just doing my job," he says. "You know, protecting the humans, as I'm supposed to do?"

"Did you attack humans?" I ask the dragon.

The magnificent form starts to shrink until it becomes the size of a man, and then it morphs into the figure of a human. A very naked human, with a shock of shaggy black hair and eyes as blue as his scales.

He's built a lot like Tristan, tall and powerful. I've become somewhat comfortable with nudity by now, with all of the shifters I live with, but I have to admit, this man makes me nervous. I turn slightly away, before Tristan catches me blushing. He just might get the wrong idea.

Ethan, the dragon shifter, answers me. "I don't know that they're humans. Not anymore. And they were coming too close."

"What do you mean?" Tristan asks.

"Some have powers. Abilities they're testing out. Too close to our nest."

"He means that new group outside Ravenbury," James clarifies. "I found him and one other blasting fire around them. The dragons were going to kill them."

The town of Ravenbury is The Loft's closest neighbors besides the dragons, run by a woman named Scout. They're friendly, and Scout and her people have never been a problem. A new group, a traveling one, had stopped nearby Ravenbury to camp a couple of blizzards ago. Travelers are usually one of two types—those still looking for a community to call home and those wanting to take over a town and make it their own. These people have done neither, promising Scout they'll move along as soon as the weather allows, but that was over a month ago, and apparently they haven't moved on yet. And apparently, they're not quite as human as I thought they were. I make a mental note to check on Ravenbury to make sure everything is okay.

"We were merely sending them along their way," Ethan says. "They do not belong here. The others, the Ravenbury people, have kept to themselves all this time. I do not trust this new group. They are encroaching on our land and water."

"They'll be on their way as soon as the snow allows them to," I say.

"Yes, well we thought we would help them along," Ethan replies. "We were not blasting them with fire, as your man here accuses, but we were melting the snow so they could move on, sooner rather than later."

"In the future, I prefer that you leave this up to me," I say.

"What do you mean when you say they have abilities and powers?" Tristan asks.

"There's one who can run nearly as fast as I can fly."

"And he's definitely Norman?" I ask.

"*She* is, yes. And there's another who's been practicing moving rocks with his mind."

27

Tristan and I exchange a look.

"Well, again, that's up to us to deal with," I say. "If you have a problem, come to me so we can avoid these kinds of situations."

"You need to keep your humans under control or we will."

I lift a brow at the threat. "No, you will not. They are not yours to deal with. And there will be consequences if you do."

Ethan growls, and smoke wisps out of his human nostrils. "You are nothing like your father."

I lift my chin and narrow my eyes. "Exactly. We *protect* the humans, not use them."

"You are still young. Wait until they start using you. Wait until these new abilities are used against you. Then you will think differently."

His words carry ancient knowledge and experience that maybe I should heed, but I still believe in humanity. And my job, my purpose, is to protect them. Even if they are changing. "Again, leave the norms to us. Otherwise, I'll allow James and his men to go dragon hunting."

Ethan leans toward me, another growl in his throat. He puffs a plume of smoke, then bursts into his dragon form, causing us all to duck to the ground, before he flies away.

"If they attack the humans again, I won't wait for your orders," James says as he rises.

Standing, I turn on him and shake a finger in his face. Well, at his throat, because I'm short and he's not. "You cannot be taking this into your own hands. Do you know what kind of trouble you could've caused all of us, including those humans?"

James growls back at me. "I'll do what I'm sworn to do. With or without your permission."

"If you start something with the dragons, you will be doing the exact opposite of what you're sworn to do. Remember your role, hunter. And don't forget that you're here on a trial basis. Consider this your only warning." I kick the tire of his ruined motorcycle. Anything with a running engine is a prized possession. With only a few motorcycles and one unreliable truck, we can't afford to lose a single vehicle. "And you'd better hope this can be fixed. It's not like we have a ton of these at our disposal. Take care of it."

With that, I stomp back inside The Loft. I try to settle down as I go down deeper, shoveling chocolate cake into my mouth as I walk, which helps lift my mood. *He's absolutely right. I am not my father. And I never will be.*

I then think about what else Ethan had said.

"Do you think norms are really gaining powers?" I ask Tristan that night once we're settled in bed. It's a nice benefit of sleeping with my second-in-command—I don't have to wait until morning when something presses on my mind.

"I don't think Ethan would lie to us."

"I don't either. Not about that. And he would know if those people were possessed. He can sense Demons. You don't think it's from the crazy weather, do you?"

"The weather?"

I sigh. "I know. It's dumb. It sounded better in my head. But seriously, what's going on with the weather? And the Demons? Owen and Vanessa have noticed on their latest travels that there seems to be a weird energy hanging over the world. Maybe that's affecting everyone?"

Tristan doesn't answer at first, and I assume he's considering all the facts. One of his abilities is being able to easily and quickly identify the best solution or options. "I'm sure the dark energy is affecting them, but my theory about the powers is that they're coming from the black magic that's probably infused into their very DNA."

I ponder this for a moment. I suppose I shouldn't have been surprised. We've already seen the black magic's effects on the flora and fauna—plants and animals aren't quite the same as they'd been before, with new, dangerous varieties popping up all the time. I suppose it was only a matter of time before we saw it in people, too.

I roll over onto my back and let out a deep sigh. "This isn't good, is it?"

"No, my love, I don't think it is. Norms with new powers will be quite dangerous. Especially to us."

I sit under the largest oak tree in our Memorial Garden to the east of The Loft's entrance, my back against the trunk as I stare up at the glass ornaments dangling from the branches. Like everything else, the Garden's been rebuilt a few times. Now, though, it's magically protected from the destructive forces, encompassing fewer trees, but each one decorated with baubles honoring a loved one we lost in the war and since. They were created by one of our mage residents who's particularly called to the fire element. She'd used her ability to make art from glass in the Before time. Now she makes items of function, molding broken glass into useful products. She once tried to teach Tristan, who can also produce fire, how to do the same, but there's actually something in this world he's not good at. His fire is apparently too hot and too direct, doing more harm than good. She lost patience with him quickly, which was fine—he has plenty of other responsibilities and she can contribute her share.

The sun has yet to peek over the horizon, but the tinge of light in the eastern sky catches the colorful glass in a way that can only be seen at this time of day. I'm not usually a morning person, especially this early, but sleep eluded me, my subconscious determined to figure out what exactly happened with that Demon—and how I should feel about it. Like everyone else, Tristan had tried to convince me there's nothing to feel guilty about when I finally had the chance to tell him about it. But I can't help it. The gruesome image won't leave my mind.

A movement at the edge of the garden grabs my attention, and my breath catches. Blinking, I tilt my head, trying to see better around another tree trunk, and when I can't, I stand, my heart doing a little stutter at the thought of who it could be. And then it sinks when I don't see anyone there.

I don't know what or who I had expected—well, yes, I do, but I don't know why. Why would I think my son would suddenly be here when it's been ten years since I last saw him? Ten years since that night I found him in this very garden, standing right where I stand now.

"Dorian?" I gasped when I realized the tall, broad stranger in the Memorial Garden was my son. The ward alarms had sounded, detecting Daemoni, and I'd been the first to arrive on the scene. I couldn't believe he'd set off the alarms —that he was Daemoni enough to do so. Tears pricked the backs of my eyes when I sent out my senses, searching for other minds in the vicinity that could have set them off and finding none. Only my son.

"Hello, Mother," he said without turning toward me, his voice deep, manly, heavy. His head was tilted slightly back, his hand raised to one of the ornaments, his finger tracing over the bracelets that decorated the glass ball.

That was Heather's ornament. I didn't need to read his mind to know the guilt he carried for his best friend's death.

"What are you doing here?" I asked. "Are you . . . back?" I dared to hope.

I hadn't seen him in six years, since the day he brought Sasha to protect his sisters. He'd all but disappeared from the world—at least, from my world, although none of my people had been able to find him, either, or even hear a peep about him from the Daemoni, as though he'd truly vanished. I'd grieved for him, knowing that even if he wasn't dead, I might have lost him forever.

But here he was.

"Back?" *he asked with a chuckle that fell flat, his arm dropping from Heather's ornament. He shoved his hands in the pockets of his suit pants and stared downward at the ground. I wanted to grab his face and make him look at me, to look in my eyes and see how much I loved him, how much I would always love him.* "Back from a special part of hell? Yes, you could say that. But not back here. I can never come back here."

"You can always—"

"No," *he growled.* "I cannot. In fact, I came to say goodbye."

"What do you mean?" *I didn't like the sound of his tone—dark and cold, final.*

"I'm not the boy you loved. Not anymore."

I rushed over to him, reaching for his arm, but he was faster than me, jerking away. "You will always be my son, Dorian. I will always love you. You can find your way back."

"No, I can't!" *The growl was more ferocious this time, and when he finally turned toward me, I flinched. A red glow filled what should have been hazel eyes—eyes just like his father's. The rest of his features were so similar and just as beautiful as Tristan's but those eyes . . . worse than even the fire that used to blaze in Tristan's. These were Daemoni eyes.*

"Dorian," *I began again.*

He shook his head, his full lips turning down into a deep frown. "I'm sorry, Mom. You have to let me go. I have to let this go." *He glanced up at the ornament once more.* "It's time to say goodbye."

"No." *I reached for him again. This time he let my hand curl over his forearm, but I gasped and jumped back at the contact. A horrible, evil energy had blasted through me. I blinked back tears, shaking my head.* "No. It's never too late."

"It is. They . . . I . . . ." *Grappling for words, he closed his eyes for a brief moment, as though trying to gather his thoughts. When he opened them, the* red glow had dimmed, but there was little life left in their depths. "The twins are in danger. What they did—it didn't go unnoticed."

"What do you mean? What did they do? In danger from whom?"

"They freed me. What they did . . . that's why I'm back. But now . . . you have to protect them."

My brows furrowed. "You're not making any sense, Dorian. What's going on with you? If you're free—"

"Not free in the way you want," he quickly corrected.

"Then what do you mean? I don't understand. What did the twins do?"

He stared at me for a moment, as though trying to figure out if I really didn't know, then shoved a hand through his hair and blew out a harsh breath. It almost seemed like he was fighting something internally. I tried to slip into his mind, but he'd built a fortress around it. It was probably one of the first things the Ancients had taught him once he became theirs.

"I have to go," he finally said. "And you have to let me."

"Dorian—"

He shook his head. "Don't. Let me go, Mom. Protect my sisters. It's too late for me, but maybe not for them."

"You know I can't let you go. I refuse to believe it's ever too late. I am here for you. I will always love you—until the end of forever."

"Until the end," he murmured, repeating the shortened version Tristan and I often told all of our children, but it almost sounded like a sneer. No, not even that. Insipid, with no feeling, no meaning.

A dark jolt shot through me as he lifted my chin with a finger, tilting my head up, forcing me to look into his eyes. And I watched as the last spark of life left them, leaving them dull, flat . . . dead.

"I'm a monster now. Don't ever forget that." And with that, he disappeared.

I haven't seen him since that night. But I've heard all the rumors. Awful, ugly tales of the worst kind. Things I would never believe my son capable of, even when he'd basically told me himself that he was.

Brushing at my face, I swipe away the wayward tear, my heart tight in my chest at the memory, at the reality. I still hold hope for Dorian. I always will.

I see the movement again, this time closer. A tall body saunters toward me.

"Owen," I breathe.

He comes to stand next to me, staring up at the ornaments overhead —at one in particular. The one hanging right next to Heather's belongs to Charlotte.

"Didn't expect to see you here," he says.

"I've been out here half the night. Too much crap in my head to sleep."

"Sounds like you need some time with Chandra."

I nod. I'd thought the same earlier. Chandra serves on my greater council. She's a were-leopard who oversees the Near East region for the Amadis. She's also a trained yogi, Reiki master, and all sorts of other things. Whenever I call a greater council meeting, which isn't often because it means pulling people from their posts all over the world, she works with me to align my chakras, balance my qi, ensure prana flow, and other good stuff that's supposed to make my life better. I admittedly don't understand it all, but I do know I always leave our sessions feeling tons calmer and more balanced.

"I think we need to call a greater council meeting anyway," I say. "I want to know if anyone else is seeing what we are with the Demons and the norms, and if so, we need to discuss."

"That's why I'm out here," he says. "Vanessa and I think we should go check things out in the communities, see what more we can learn about both."

With Owen's portal-making skills, he and Vanessa travel all over, visiting other communities around the world to gather information, find out their needs, and deliver resources. Our bird-shifters still serve as a network to deliver messages, but Owen and Vanessa are our primary liaisons with the rest of the world. I know, who would have ever thought Vanessa could be a diplomat? Owen's more laid-back demeanor counterbalances her sharper, more assertive one, but sometimes that's needed, too. They actually make a really good team—and a perfect couple, which I never thought I'd say, but it's true. They're each other's yin and yang.

I nod again. "Absolutely. I was going to hold a core council meeting today to discuss everything that happened yesterday and send you two off to see what you can find out."

"We're ready to go now, if that's cool with you. See you in a couple of weeks?"

I consider this for a brief moment. "Two weeks, but that's all. We really do need to hold a greater council meeting sooner than later. We're way overdue."

"Two weeks, then." He touches a finger to his lips and then to his mother's ornament before striding off. I wave at Vanessa, who's standing at the gate, waiting for him.

After they leave, I lift my hand to cup Char's ornament. I miss her so much. I miss them all, my heart aching for her and my mom and my grandmother. I could really use their advice about now, but it's been years since I've seen or heard from them. They used to bring me messages from the Angels, but not anymore. I've assumed it's because we haven't needed them—that we've been doing everything right, since they only come when their interference is necessary for the greater good.

After yesterday's events, though, doubt is creeping in.

I hadn't mentioned it to Owen, but I hadn't just come out here to this particular place because I couldn't sleep. I'd been hoping that maybe Mom or Rina would have come for a visit. After all, I might have killed a human. I'd think that worth some interference. But alas, if they heard me calling out for them in the dark, they haven't responded. This is the real reason I want to go to Amadis Island, not only for a greater council meeting or to work with Chandra.

I just really kind of want my mom and the rest of my ancestors right now. Some information would be nice, but also some reassurance that everything will be okay.

Because I have a knotted feeling in the pit of my stomach that absolutely nothing is okay.

"$\mathcal{S}$o we all agree that something's going on. We just don't know what." I glance around at my core council after hearing the few reports they've been able to gather in the last couple of weeks.

I still haven't been able to reach my mother or grandmother or to reveal the book that's supposed to deliver messages from the Angels when they don't send Mom or Rina. The book is magical, kept in the Otherworld, I assume, because it only appears when necessary. I tried to assure myself as I always have—no contact means everything is fine. More and more these last couple of weeks, though, doubt about that has bloomed.

"Whatever it is out there, it's dark as Hell," Vanessa says. Rather than taking a seat in a chair behind one of the tables of the conference room, she sits on the table, her long, leather-clad legs crossed and swinging. Her ice-blue eyes glance at Owen before returning to me. "And trust me, I know dark."

She and Owen had returned from gathering intelligence yesterday morning and haven't had time to brief my small council before they left with me to check on Ravenbury and the group Ethan had been so worried about. It's been two weeks since the dragon incident, and the group is still there. Ethan's patience is surely growing thin.

"Everywhere we went, people seem to be more on edge than ever. More aggressive. Shorter tempers," Owen adds. "That nasty energy feels almost tangible, like a blanket settling over communities. If it grows, it could be just as bad as after the bombs."

Vanessa crosses her pale arms and makes a face of disgust. "Worse. I swear it feels worse, if that's even possible.

Great. Not at all what I want to hear. I'd hoped the feeling I'd experienced that day had simply been intuition for the events that followed with the Demons and the dragons. But the sensation hadn't gone away after, and apparently I'm not the only one who's been feeling it. So what the hell is going on?

Jax, the Australian were-crocodile and Blossom's mate, speaks up. "It must be the Daemoni up to something."

I shake my head. "I don't think so. They're still not in a place to do something as big as this."

"We don't know what place they're in," Aidan says with a heavy Scottish accent. He's a post-war addition to my council, a gargoyle who had been stuck in his rock form on the side of a church for centuries until after the war. Sheree helped him get unstuck so that he could maintain his human form and shift at will as he used to. They became a thing and have been together ever since. Aidan has been a great source of old history of the supernaturals—beyond even Tristan and Vanessa, who date back to the 1700s—so I'd added him to the council.

"I didn't mean geographically," I mutter, although Aidan's claim is true. The Daemoni keep their main sites cloaked. We've found a few clusters, nests, covens, and packs scattered about, but we still haven't been able to find their HQ—their new Hades, as it had been called before, where the Ancients reside. As well as my son, their leader. And I definitely have my people on the hunt.

"Nor did I," Aidan says. "It's been sixteen years since they lost the war. They've surely increased their numbers, probably easier than ever because nobody can track the dead anymore, with those zombies out there. And they have help from dragons and others freed from Hell, thanks to you."

"Careful," Tristan warns at the accusatory edge in Aidan's last sentence. "Those creatures that had been held captive in Hell didn't all deserve to be there."

"The dragons did," Aidan says. "And they're not the only ones."

Aidan and the dragons, I think with a sigh. Aidan doesn't trust the dragons any further than he can throw them. They had a long cross-species feud that went back to the creation of the gargoyles many centuries ago. When Aidan found out Tristan and I, with the help of a few fae, had freed the dragons from Hell, along with other creatures that had disappeared from Earth, he'd thrown a gargoyle-worthy fit. Of course, if not for that series of events, he'd still have been stuck to that church and would have never met Sheree, whom he now claims to be the love of his life he thought he'd never find. He's never come around to the dragons, not even the nearby clan that has been somewhat friendly . . . in relative terms.

"We've seen nothing that shows the Daemoni strong enough to be behind all this," Sheree says. "I'm with Alexis on this. Sorry, babe."

Aidan attempts a scowl, but I don't miss the wink he gives Sheree. My heart does a little happy dance. Everyone deserves a love like mine and Tristan's, especially someone as special as Sheree.

Blossom nods, though her eyes are filled with sadness. "Even if they were strong enough, I just don't see Dorian allowing this. I don't care what everyone else says about him."

"It wouldn't be up to Dorian," Vanessa says. "It'd be up to the Ancients."

I know, too, that the Ancients *are* powerful, but are they powerful enough? If so, why are they acting only now? If they have this kind of power to create the kind of dark energy Vanessa and Owen have described, they wouldn't need the Daemoni as their army. They wouldn't need to rebuild before acting. They could have done this years ago. Hell, millennia ago. And they certainly wouldn't have needed to take my son to do it. Tristan voices these same thoughts to the group—minus the last one, too personal to bring into the discussion.

"Okay, so we have some kind of growing dark energy, norms who seem to be evolving, and the Demon issue," I say, moving on to our next topic.

"Maybe it's all related. Maybe it's not the Daemoni behind it all, but the Demons themselves," Carlie suggests. I'd brought my old college friend onto the small council for her medical expertise and her Norman perspective, but even now, she doesn't have the same experience with the Demons as the rest of us. She's seen the physical damage one can do to a body, but as our doctor, she's never been out fighting the Demons herself. She tugs at her short blond hair when we all look at her in shock, and she shrugs.

"They aren't smart enough to organize like this," I dismiss with a snort.

"Except we did hear more reports of possessions," Vanessa says.

"And not just possessions," Owen adds. "People are *acting* like they're possessed, but nobody's sensing the Demons."

"Like the ones we encountered last month," Sheree says.

"Yeah," I say distantly as I recall the events. "Like the woman, but . . . we have to figure out what the deal was with the other." I swallow, a lump in my throat. "The human."

"He was a Demon, Alexis," Owen says firmly. "I don't doubt it."

"Neither do I," Vanessa and Sheree say at the same time.

"You shouldn't either, Alexis," Sheree continues. "Even if the human had been evolving or gaining powers or whatever, there's no doubt there was a Demon in him."

"Or maybe not in him," Ragan pipes up. "The she-Demon could have been throwing dark magic on him to look like your typical Demon so you'd kill him. If she was more powerful than him."

I cock my head as I look at the blonde hunter. I'd added her to my core council not long after she and her boyfriend Ryder had come to The Loft and she'd quickly proven herself as a natural leader. Like me, she's petite but strong, driven by her purpose. "What do you mean? Do you know something about these new kinds of Demons?"

"I think I might. And they're definitely not new," she says. "So you know the old woman in the bayou I told you about? The one who summoned us to become hunters and oversaw our training? You guys think she's some sort of mage since she endowed us with some powers."

"Yeah, I remember you telling us about her," I say. Nobody had known about supernatural hunters until the war had begun, but apparently they've been out there for years, perhaps decades. We'd run into our first one in Russia, and then met a whole group of them in Washington, D.C., one of whom was James, an old acquaintance of mine. Eventually, Ragan and her group found us at The Loft. Once I added her to the council and she knew we could be trusted, she'd explained the origins of the hunters to us—an old woman in Louisiana who had bestowed some basic powers to those she thought worthy. Mostly, they're just very well trained, equal to the most elite soldiers of the Normans, but they also have the ability to recognize the supernatural among the humans, and some extra strength and speed.

"Well, she taught us a lot about the Demons. We weren't only supposed to hunt what we now know are the Daemoni. We were trained to hunt Demons, too."

"But that was before Lucas punctured the veil," I say. "You said you'd been hunters for years before then."

Ragan nods. "We were. And there were Demons in our physical realm then—and long, long before. Forever, I guess. Just not so obvious."

Tristan strokes his jaw. "The Ancients mentioned other Demons roaming Earth. They didn't speak of them much, though. There was definitely sibling rivalry with them."

"Mom and Rina alluded to the same thing, saying the Rule of Demons was much longer than they cared to admit," I say, recalling when they'd visited us after the twins were born. When they'd told me the Rule of Demons was over, and this is now the Age of Angels. "They were in hiding, though, not flying around like they do now."

"Hiding in human bodies," Ragan clarifies. "Moving from body to body as the need struck—still strikes. All imperceptible by most. Definitely by humans. The magic the woman gave us allowed us to perceive the evil in the Daemoni and to detect some Demons in human bodies. But she said there were others—Higher and Major Demons—that we had to be careful of. The Majors are the greatest deceivers, practically undetectable, and therefore the most dangerous."

"So there's a hierarchy of Demons." I rub the back of my neck. "That makes sense. The Angels have a hierarchy, from the Archangels down to us, Earth's Angels. And since the Demons used to be Angels, I guess they'd keep some kind of organization."

"Right, and the ones we can see and have been sending back to Hell are probably the lowest—the Lessers."

I let out a kind of snort. "So those fugly, horned, mottle-skinned things that we can see are the Demon equivalents to the Earth's Angels? But they're so dumb!"

"Or they *act* dumb," Tristan suggests.

Ragan's blue gaze bounces between us. "Do you get what I'm saying? There are other Highers still here. There have always been, coming and going, finding humans willing to give up their souls or whose souls are already so dark, they're basically open doors to these guys. And possibly Majors, who don't even need a human suit. They can take human form all on their own."

"So we have a major Demon problem," I say.

"A major problem with Major Demons," Owen clarifies.

I can't help but wonder why this has never been mentioned before. *Why haven't the Angels ever brought this to our attention, now or in the past?* Surely they've known about it.

"How did this old woman know so much about Demons?" Vanessa asks. "I mean, Tristan and I were in the inner circle of the Ancients, and we don't know this much."

"She could have been one," Tristan suggests. "Possibly an Ancient—a rogue sorceress who took off to do her own thing for one reason or another."

"Why would an Ancient want the Daemoni—their own army—hunted and killed, though?" I ask.

"Not all were in agreement about creating the Daemoni or how it was done, especially the sorcerers," Tristan replies. "Many detest the vampires and even the lower mages. Seems like she may have been building her own army."

"And don't forget—not all sorcerers and mages originated with the Ancients," Blossom chimes in.

That had been another revelation we'd discovered—the Ancients hadn't created all of the supernatural species in our world, as we'd all been taught. We'd been lied to. I can't think about that right now, though, because it would only frustrate me further.

"So why would she want to protect the humans?" I ask. "I mean, that's why she created the hunters, right? To kill the Daemoni?"

"Daemoni, Demons, yes, that was, *is*, our primary objective," Ragan says. "But does it matter right now? My point is that Demons don't need the Gates of Hell to be open to come and go as they please. All they need are humans with enough darkness to attract them. And the humans still left in this world live in desperate times."

"And desperation brings out the worst in everyone," Carlie says.

"So our world is probably crawling with Demons—more than we imagined." I suppress a groan—and the urge to kick the wall.

"The question is, what do we do about this infestation?" Aidan asks.

"I, for one, would like to talk to this old woman," I say, dropping my hands to my waist and tapping my fingers on my hips. "I'd like to know what else she knows. We need all the help we can get. Do you think she survived and she's still in the bayou?"

"I bet yes," Ragan answers. "She's a tough old bitch. The question is whether she'll let us find her."

"She won't come to her own? To you?"

Ragan averts her eyes and gnaws on her bottom lip for a moment before her gaze returns to me. "I don't know. Before everything went down we were warned, practically threatened, to stay clear of the Amadis. She said it was for our own good—that you guys wouldn't appreciate us killing those who may still have hope in your eyes—but . . . I question her motives now more than ever. And she's not one I want pissed off at me, if you know what I mean."

"What if you, Ryder, and a few other hunters go without us? Without any supes at all?" I ask.

"I doubt she'll tell us any more than she already has."

"You never know. It's been a long time, and everything is different now. Everyone's perspective and therefore their motives have changed," Tristan says.

"And if you don't get anything, at least you can let us know if she's still there and we can investigate," I add. "If anything, we need to know who and what she is."

"We'll need some supplies and bikes," Ragan replies. "And I'm *not* taking James."

I smile. "I can't bribe you with anything?"

"There's not a thing you can give me in this world that would make spending several weeks with him worth it."

My smile becomes a frown. "Let's hope it won't take that long."

"Well, she'll detect a portal's magic, so we have to drive down there, which means hunting for fuel and supplies on the way and walking if we run out or break down." And the chances for those happening are high, considering the state of our vehicles and that they'll have to take a special potion Owen created to make the stale fuel work—if they even find any. Ragan continues, "There's also the matter of finding her current den, which could be anywhere in the South, and then hopefully, making it back."

That groan of frustrations creeps up on me again, nearly escaping. What seems like the simplest task takes twenty times longer and with a hundred times more effort than it used to. Oh, how I miss the days of gas stations and convenience stores every few miles, airplanes, and cell phones.

"You're sure she'll have a problem with magical protection? Like a cloak and shield so you at least don't have to deal with the gangs? I hate sending you all off practically naked."

"The magic she gave us is all the protection we need. And it did us well for all those years before we ever hooked up with you."

I sigh reluctantly. "Okay. I don't like it, but I'm sure you're right. You can start making plans when we're done here. I'd like you to leave as soon as possible." I look around at the rest of my council. "In the meantime, we need to get more aggressive with the Demons we do know about, and we need to find out where they, and all this dark energy, is coming from. How it's getting into *our* world."

"And then we need to shut that shit down," Vanessa says.

I nod. "Exactly."

"And just when things were going fairly well," Sheree laments with a sigh.

I understand her frustration. We'd recently been able to settle a major peace treaty between two large factions in Eastern Europe, on the heels of another that had been agreed to among three communities in what had been Japan. We're still far from worldwide peace, but there hasn't been a major war in over sixteen years. My goal all along has been to avoid any more war. We aren't supposed to meddle in human affairs, but that's my hard line. We've all survived enough war for more than a lifetime, as far as I'm concerned.

"Vanessa and Owen, get the word out that I'm calling a greater council meeting in three weeks," I say. "Make sure everyone knows our primary topic, so they're prepared to discuss it. Hopefully we can get some concrete information. We need to know more before we can decide what to do about all of this."

Vanessa swings herself to her feet and pegs me with an icy glare. "But when the time comes, we *will* do something about it, right?"

My brows pinch together. "Of course. That's what we do."

Vanessa eyes me for a long moment. "As long as you remember that. There might come a time you actually have to use that power you've been given. And it looks like that time is coming."

I shrug. "Only if necessary, sister. Don't forget our directive."

"A directive from those who appear to have abandoned us." Vanessa raises a brow, challenging me to deny her theory. Of course, I can't. She knows how long it's been since they've been in communication.

42

I hope the Angels haven't truly abandoned us, but I know she's right. This dark energy isn't about the humans anyway, and the time may be coming to show the Demons and the Daemoni who's still in charge here. My ultimate directive is to protect humanity and this world, and if that means another war against evil, then so be it.

CHAPTER 5

"*Y*ou really don't want to go to Amadis Island with us?" I ask the twins at dinner a few weeks later, the night we're leaving for the greater council meeting.

"Definitely sure," Elliana replies before shoveling a forkful of macaroni and cheese into her mouth.

"Yeah, I'd rather stay here," Brielle says, which surprises me more than Elli's response. The girls used to love going to the island and exploring the ruins of what had once been a thriving settlement and the headquarters of the Amadis before the Daemoni destroyed it at the beginning of the war. They always returned with pockets full of treasures, some of real value and some nothing more than seashells or colorful rocks. Elliana lost interest before Brielle had. In fact, this is her first time not even considering it.

"Oh, so you have big plans now?" Tristan teases. "I thought this place was boring."

"Well, you know, the new kid, Corbin, makes moonshine and we're having a big party," Elli quips with an eyeroll. Her father lifts a brow, which only eggs her on. "I plan to get . . . how do you say it? Totally garbaged."

I snort-laugh. The fact that she doesn't know the words wasted or trashed in this sense comforts me, that along with a few other things giving away that she's being her usual sarcastic self. I know, however, that it's only a matter of time before Elli does come home drunk or high or both. Brielle, probably not, at least not until she's much older. But Elli's our rebel and daredevil, the one to push limits. I could only hope that she goes through the *Ang'dora* first, which would prevent her from getting "garbaged" because her cells would regenerate too fast to be affected.

Of course, we don't know if the girls will even experience the *Ang'dora*, the enigmatic change my kind goes through to receive our gifts from the Angels, at least not in the traditional sense. The *Ang'dora's* like an awakening, when all of the magic given to us by the various types of supernatural creatures embedded in our DNA reveals itself with a turbo-boost of power from the Angels. The girls' powers have already begun manifesting, though, weak as they are and mostly mage-oriented, so far. Blossom's been teaching them simple protective charms, spells, and potions. They sprouted their wings shortly after birth, but Mom and Rina had hidden them, not to come out since. That same power might be suppressing the rest of their abilities until they're old enough to control them. I don't know how much longer that magic will hold, though. We don't know what to expect at all with the twins. Everything had changed with their father and me, and there's nothing like them or their brother on this Earth. Our entire family is an anomaly.

"Actually, Dad," Brielle says, as she leans forward a bit, toward her father, "Aunt Blossom has a list of plants she needs foraged out in the woods. She thought we could help Charleigh with it tomorrow while you're gone."

Elliana remains quiet, pretending to be engrossed in her food, while Brielle looks imploringly at Tristan. The two have a closer bond than Elli does with him—with either of us, really. Tristan and Brielle are like two peas in a pod in many ways, both analytically minded. In fact, one of the abilities we think Brie might have is being able to see solutions easily, like Tristan can. She's also numbers-oriented like her father. With so many similar interests, they've spent a lot of time together, while Elli prefers to train physically or hang out with her "Aunt Nessa." When Vanessa's not around, I'll often find her in The Loft's library, pouring over books we've managed to collect and salvage. She's not a book nerd in the same sense Brielle and I are. Elli reads specific kinds of non-fiction, either about combat and war-heroes, or about exploration, geography, and the like. If ever given the opportunity, she'll be the first to run off for the promise and allure of an adventure.

Apparently, Amadis Island is no longer much of an adventure to her.

"What do you think, Lex?" Tristan asks me.

Chewing the bite of bread I'd just taken, I consider the request. "I don't know that it's a good idea. All of our best protectors will be with us. And there's still that group near Ravenbury."

"They left last week." As soon as Tristan says it, I remember Aidan telling me this news. He and Sheree had done a run to Ravenbury and the surrounding areas, which conveniently includes the lake where the dragons reside. The gargoyle never misses an opportunity to check on the dragon clan, to make sure they're not burning down villages or eating babies or whatever memories and stories he recalls from a different era many centuries ago. I don't know if he'll ever completely accept that times have changed and maybe the dragons have, too.

"Besides, we'll stay within the ward's boundaries, so nobody will see us. And Sasha will be with us, too," Brielle says. "You know we can't be any safer."

"You would be with us on Amadis Island," I say half-heartedly. I'm already resigned that they won't be going.

"Promise to stay within the wards?" Tristan asks.

"Pinky swear," both girls say, lifting their hands with their little fingers raised. He indulges their pinky-shakes, although we both know that their most highly regarded solemn oath is one they only do with each other and Charleigh.

"Don't do anything stupid if you want to see your next birthday," Tristan says, as his little fingers twine around theirs.

"That's in three days," Brielle says, as if we need to be reminded. Sweet Sixteen doesn't mean what it once did, but they haven't stopped talking about the upcoming milestone.

"Exactly." Tristan lifts a brow, eyeing each of them. They both nod as their fingers curl tighter and they do the swear.

"Can we be excused so we can go tell Charleigh?" Brielle asks sweetly.

Tristan leans back in his chair, crosses his thick arms over his broad chest, and eyes them. I watch him just as carefully, wondering what he's up to.

"Wait, I want you to pinky swear further," he says.

"On what?"

"No boys." His gaze lingers on Brielle for a moment but then settles more heavily on Elliana. "Promise me no boys until you're at least thirty. No kissing, not even handholding. And definitely no drinking with them. Pinky swear on that."

I'm a bit taken aback as he speaks, but I watch Elliana for her reaction. Her face goes from pink to a bright red to a dark crimson as her brows lower with each word. She knows this is directed specifically to her, which doesn't make any sense to either of us. She suddenly bursts out of her seat, her good mood gone as she explodes.

"Seriously, Dad! Gods! Do you even know me at all?" She doesn't wait for a response, but marches off as fast as her legs can take her, Brielle scurrying after her.

Tristan looks at me with complete bewilderment as I stand. "What? They're way too young for that shit."

"First of all, consider who their parents are. And then their aunt Vanessa and the rest of their extended family. Do you really think boys are going to randomly try to hook up with them? They're all scared to death of us!" He starts to grin until I continue. "But more importantly—are you *seriously* that clueless?"

Like my daughter, I don't wait for an answer. I hurry after her, wondering how my insanely intelligent, observant, and considerate husband who's always been an amazing father could be so damn oblivious. Of course, I only have a gut feeling myself, reinforced by a few snippets of thoughts I'd picked up here and there—neither of the girls have shown much interest in romance yet, never even talking about it except to tease each other. It's not like there's been any opportunity, considering there are only four other teens in The Loft, including Charleigh and the new kid Corbin.

By the time I reach our apartment, Charleigh's already with the twins in their room, and they shoo me away. I give them some time, but then I order Charleigh and Brielle out so I can talk to my daughter. Elli's in her bed, curled up under the covers, sniffling.

"Hey," I quietly say as I sit next to her. "Do you want to talk about it?"

"There's nothing to talk about." Her tone is harsh, but I can hear the tears in her voice, feel the pain she's trying to hide.

"Are you sure?" I gently prod.

"I'm sure. Just leave me alone. I'll be fine."

I sit for a few minutes, both of us silent, besides her occasional sniffling. Elli's not a crier, not like me, so I know she's really hurting. I can't blame her, but on the other hand, she's been keeping things to herself that she shouldn't be. I don't want to push her until she's ready, but I hate knowing she's in pain when it's so needless.

"Well, you know I love you, no matter what," I say. "I always will, until the end."

She inhales a shuddering breath, then suddenly sits up and throws herself against me. My arms wrap around her automatically, holding her as she cries into my shoulder.

"Thanks, Mom," she finally whispers after my shirt is soaked and her sobs have slowed.

"You're sure you don't want to talk about it?" I ask one more time as I smooth her hair down her back.

"I'm sure. Not now. I'm just . . . it's just stupid hormones, I guess. I'll be fine."

"Of course, you will. You're my daughter. You'll be more than fine. But even the strongest warriors and greatest leaders have needs, you know. Like the need to get things off their chests?"

Her grip on me tightens, but she doesn't say anything. I accept that she's still not ready.

"Until the end," I whisper again as I hold her.

"Until the end," she replies quietly against my shoulder.

"Are you going to tell me what that was all about?" Tristan asks later while we wait on my core council to gather in our meeting room. Amadis Island is halfway around the world, where it's already morning. Owen and Vanessa have been gone for hours, opening portals for my greater council members scattered around the world. They should all be there by now, waiting only on us.

"It's not for me to tell," I say, shrugging. My black leather fighting gear—standard for any kind of travel outside the wards—shifts and creaks with the movement.

"*Ma lykita?*" He steps in front of where I lean against a table, blocking my view of everything so that I have to look up at him. Not that it's a bad view—especially when he's also donning black leather and weapons. Damn, he's sexy. "Are we good?"

My heart softens as I gaze into his eyes, and I smile. "Of course, we are."

"But you're still going to keep this secret from me?"

I sigh. "It's not my secret. In fact, she hasn't even told me. I'm just observant—for once, more observant than you, apparently."

He scowls, not liking this, but he seems to accept it for now, because his expression morphs into concern. "Is she going to be okay, at least? Or will she hate me forever now?"

"Not even Elli can hate you forever. But it wouldn't hurt for you to apologize."

"I don't know what I'm apologizing for."

"Just go apologize for hurting her, even if it was unintentional. If anything, just blame it on being a man. Trust me—she'll be good with that."

He studies me for a long moment, as though he doesn't believe me, but then strides off, back toward our apartment. I'm glad he wants to do this before we leave. We'd learned the hard way with Dorian to never take tomorrow for granted.

At the same time he returns, Sheree and Aidan hurry into the room, the last to arrive. We walk up the tunnel together and outside beyond the boundaries, where Owen's already waiting for us. I've been hoping Ragan and her hunters would have returned by now with news to take to the meeting, but we haven't heard a peep from them since they left.

As soon as I pass through the portal, I'm greeted by my advisors with warm hugs and smiles. We celebrate our reunion after nearly a year of not gathering with a meal on the hill where the Council Hall used to stand, then buckle down to business.

None of the reports bring good news or enlightenment. Demons are changing. So are the norms. And everyone feels this same dark energy settling over our world.

"Tell me exactly what you mean," I say. I know what we've been feeling in our part of the world, but is it the same everywhere?

"It feels like hatred," Chandra answers from her perch on a broken marble column that's been magically smoothed into a seat.

Jelani, my representative from Africa, nodded. "A lot of tension, like everyone's ready for a fight."

"Despair and dread," my uncle Noah adds. Another Earth Angel, he helps me manage this part of the world, and everyone knows to go to him if anything were to happen to both Tristan and me. He's nearly as big as Tristan, with long dark hair, a face that can sometimes be terrifying with its hard edges and the scar through his sharply angled eyebrow, and it's kind of odd to hear him describe it, especially when he continues. "And for some, it's like the worst kind of sadness that shrivels the heart and darkens the soul. Suicide rates are at their worse since the war."

"If we don't find the source of it, I'm afraid war will be imminent," Chandra says, her voice soft and heavy.

Jelani agrees. "The question is—with the Demons or the Daemoni or both again?"

And I can't help but wonder if it's something even worse.

CHAPTER 6

*D*ark waves crash against the rocks at the bottom of the cliff at the northern end of Amadis Island, sending a spray of foam high up into the air. The island, among many that spread out from the coastline of what was once known as Greece, is unlike any of the others, undetectable by human eyes for over two millennia. Well, it was up until the war, anyway. Now it's a pile of rubble and ruins. I stand at the cliff's edge several hundred yards above the rocks and the Aegean Sea below, my hair blowing in the breeze and salty drops peppering my face. I raise my arms out from my body, let my head fall back, and close my eyes. With a deep breath, I spring off the edge and quietly descend.

A thrill jolts through me, starting in my belly. My shoulders and spine prickle with an instinctual need to save myself, but I refuse to give in, reveling in the sensation of the freefall. About a third of the way down, I arc my body and swing myself toward the cliff wall, landing gracefully on the ledge that juts out from a shallow cave. Only then do I allow my wings to burst free.

Closing them against my back, I stand and gaze at the interior wall, my eyes scanning over the many female faces burnt into the rocky surface —the images of my ancestors, the past matriarchs of the Amadis. Their likenesses have been emblazoned onto the stone by their funeral pyres that had been sent over the cliff's edge over the last two millennia. I brush my fingers over the newest ones, a frown pulling down my brow and lips. Are my eyes playing tricks or are all of the images fading?

After one last look, I turn to face the sea and drop to sit cross-legged at the ledge's edge, curving my wings around me until all I can see is the sea before me. I focus on the waves close to the horizon, letting their rise and fall mesmerize me and relax my mind. I match my breaths to the rhythm, inhaling the salty air, ignoring the sprays from below. I want to tune out all of the mind signatures at the other end of the island and silence the many voices in my head—the number one problem with being a telepath. In a few moments, though, I'll be able to erect my wall and quiet my mind, but I need to wait for Chandra.

Our council meeting ended about thirty minutes ago, and I could finally have some time with her before we return home. I really, really need this and hope like hell she can help me find balance.

My mind tugs toward my leadership role and responsibilities. My warrior soul wants to fight, to protect my people and my world. And my heart . . . my heart ceaselessly yearns for more time with Tristan and the girls. Because there's just never enough. Life has clearly proven that. Achieving any level of balance is a pipe dream, I know. So, really, my work with Chandra is in admitting and finding acceptance that regardless of my inhuman abilities and powers, I'll never be Super Mom. She's been trying to help me realize this for over a decade now. She has the patience of a saint.

Even as I sit now, gazing out at the sea and trying to relax, my mind wanders in a hundred different directions. I hate the thought of another war. I'd hoped my girls and their entire generation—and the one after it too—would never know its ugliness, especially as young as they still are. I'd hoped the rest of us would never experience it again. Perhaps I should know better than to think peace would last forever, but I'd do whatever necessary to prolong it for as long as possible.

As I think about the council meeting, another part of my mind wanders to the far side of the island, where the Amadis village once stood and where Tristan is now with other council members, trying to narrow down details about rebuilding the village. Amadis Island had been one of the very first targets of the Daemoni. We'd been debating for years whether to rebuild the island. The Loft is home, but Amadis Island is sacred and a connection to the past. This is the main reason I was disappointed that the girls have lost interest in it. Now, though, as issues seem to be escalating, it's becoming increasingly clear that we may once again need this home-base for the Amadis and a refuge for those unable to fight.

I close my eyes and practice what Chandra has taught me about meditating, but until I can erect my mental wall, it's pointless. But doing so—cutting my mind off from the outside world—makes everyone here on the island vulnerable because I'm their first line of defense. I can detect anyone heading our way even before their supernatural senses can. Not that we have any enemies we can't handle, but with my full council in one place, they are a valuable target for the few who would dare try. Besides, I haven't forgotten what Ragan said about the Demons—about Major Demons roaming our Earth.

I imagine that thought floating away, like a cloud in the sky, not something to hold on to now, and bring my mind back to center. Then Chandra's voice pops into my head.

"*I am up here.*" Like everyone's, her mental voice holds the same qualities as her vocal one, soft and lilting with the slightest touch of a big cat's roar marking the animal inside her. "*Most of the others left. We're being guarded so you can take a break.*"

That's what I've been waiting to hear. I stand and turn for one last look at my ancestors, including my mom and grandmother. My heart sinks. The images, created by Angel magic, are most definitely fading.

I leap off the edge and fly up to the top of the cliff for our session. I sort of want to take Chandra down to the ledge to be closer to the previous Amadis matriarchs, but that space is sacred and only reserved for the matriarchs themselves. The Sacred Archives, another hallowed space, used to reside in the matriarch's mansion, but that had been demolished. We've yet to find any evidence of what had happened to the Sacred Archives—the room or the books it housed. I've always believed it's a small pocket of the Otherworld the matriarchs are allowed to enter, so I hope someone on the other side had merely sealed it off from this plane of existence when the mansion fell.

The Indian woman already sits cross-legged near the edge of the cliff, her long, black hair in a braid that cords down her silk-clad back. She gives me a warm smile that reaches her large, almond-shaped dark eyes and reveals teeth a bright white against the deep golden color of her skin. I've never seen Chandra in her leopard form, but knowing what to look for, I can see the tilt of a cat's eyes and points on her teeth that hint at fangs rather than normal human teeth.

Retracting my wings, I drop in front of Chandra, mirroring her position.

"Ready?" she asks.

"*Ready?*" I call out to the others to make sure they're in place to guard the island while I turn my thoughts off to everyone.

"*Ready, my love,*" Tristan replies. "*We'll be fine.*"

I nod to Chandra. "We're good to go."

Then I close my eyes and imagine a thick, black wall that encloses Chandra and me within, blocking out everyone else's thoughts. Except for meditating, I haven't needed to use this wall since the early days of receiving the gift of telepathy, when the wall had been my coping mechanism. I'd needed it while learning how to control the intrusion of others' thoughts in my head. Then I'd learned to disintegrate the wall into a screen that serves as a filter of all of those thoughts, allowing me more control over which ones I hear. But as the only telepath in this world, my mind is often used as Central Station, a hub for everyone's thoughts to pass through to each other. My brain allows communication when it'd normally be impossible because of distance or the need for stealth, considering cell phones and texting are things of the past.

There had come a point, though, when all of the traffic through my head became an issue. Tristan had insisted I do something about it before I had a breakdown. Then Chandra helped me realize how useful my old wall could be when I need downtime. Actually, admitting when I need downtime, and then asking for it, has proven to be a completely different challenge.

With eyes closed, we focus inwardly. Chandra guides the meditation, using images rather than words. We mentally travel through lights and colors until settling into a peaceful state. When thoughts about Demons or the most recent argument with the twins start filling my mind, Chandra gently nudges me back to center. Eventually, I feel as though I'm drifting away.

"Alexis." The woman's voice comes as a whisper at first but grows louder. "Alexis!"

"*Mom?*" I gasp, elation filling me at finally hearing my mother's voice for the first time in so long.

I open my eyes and find myself not on the cliff top of Amadis Island, but in a blank space of only whiteness and fog. No floor, no ceiling, no walls. Only a seemingly unending space of white light. I've been here before, a long time ago: I'm just outside of Heaven's Gates. Curling wisps of fog retreat, and my mother stands in front of me. We could have been twins, but her wings are a pearly white and her facial features seem a few years older than my appearance of about twenty Earth years.

Mom steps forward and grabs my hands with urgency. Fear shines in her eyes. I frown. My mother rarely shows fear. "Honey, they're calling us in."

"What do you mean?"

"The matriarchs. We all have to go."

My brows pinch together. "Where are we going?"

Mom shakes her head as her eyes fill with tears. "I'm sorry, honey, but not you. The rest of us."

"What? You're leaving me? Us? But—"

"I know what has been promised to you, but everything has changed. It's all up to you now."

"Sophia, hurry!" The voice of my grandmother, Rina, rings with intense urgency through the whiteness before she emerges from the fog. "Come, Sophia." She looks my way, and while the corners of her mouth turn down, I can see fear in her eyes. "I am sorry, Alexis, but we must go. There's no time to waste!"

Her fear washes over me, causing my heart rate to accelerate. "But why? What's going on? Tell me!"

"I'm sorry, honey," Mom says. "There's no time. Just be ready."

"Ready for what?"

"The Gates are closing!" Rina frantically pulls on Mom's arm.

"Wait!" I cry out. "What Gates? Heaven's?"

Neither answer. Their images fade into the fog.

Mom's voice floats through but drifts away. "It's coming, Alexis. The twins are at risk. Protect them at all costs. Don't let the darkness find them. Or all realms will fall."

Anything else my mother might have said is overpowered by a great clang that reverberates all around me, shaking the Otherworld and making my very bones rattle. I gasp as my hand flies to my throat.

"No!"

"*Alexis.*" The familiar female voice with the thick accent calls out. Not my mother's or grandmother's or anyone else's in the Otherworld. No. Chandra. Right. The vision seems so real, I've forgotten I'd been meditating. "*Alexis, are you okay?*"

I open my eyes, blinking against the bright afternoon sunlight. Chandra stares at me with concern.

"What happened?" she asks. "You disengaged."

Staring at the ground between us but still seeing the white fog—still hearing that metallic clang echoing in my ears—I frown. "I'm not quite sure. My mom and Rina . . ."

That sound hadn't really been Heaven's Gates closing, had it? This isn't how they normally visit me to provide counsel and guidance—when they used to bother at all. Only once had they taken me to the Otherworld, to the front of Heaven's Gates. They normally came to my world. Had this even been real? Or had it only been a meditative dream?

If there's nothing to it, I don't want to alarm Chandra. Not yet. I'll have to find out more, but when I'm alone. I hope I can reach them this time.

"I saw them," I finally finish. "In a dream state, anyway."

Chandra smiles, pleased. "Good. You broke away from the real world for a bit and visited with your ancestors. They're always around when we need them. We only have to quiet our minds and *feel* for them. This session was good, yes?"

I return her grin with a forced one. After all, that wasn't what I would call a nice visit with my ancestors, as much as I really do want to talk to them. "Yes. This was great. Thank you, Chandra. You probably need to get going. We all have business to take care of."

I hope that doesn't sound too rudely dismissive, but I need to be alone as soon as possible. I drop the wall in my mind, notifying the others that I'm back online, so to speak, so they can be on their way to their homes. Most of them anyway. My core team will wait for me.

We both stand and hug, then Chandra disappears with a faint *pop* of air. As soon as I'm alone, I jump down to the cave on the side of the cliff, close my eyes, and call for my ancestors.

"I need your help, Mom! Rina!" I wait impatiently for them to appear. "Cassandra? Anybody?" I pause again, although I don't really expect Cassandra, the first matriarch of the Amadis, to come. She's only done so once or twice before. Mom and Rina usually serve as the Angels' liaisons. "Mom, please! It's important!"

None of them appear, but that doesn't necessarily mean anything. They don't exactly stand by, waiting for my beck and call. If they had, I'd be calling for them all the time because I miss them so much and hate that my daughters are growing up without their Mimi. In fact, if it were up to me, I'd just keep Mom here in the Earthly realm all the time. No, they usually only come when *they* decide. They being the Heavenly Host.

So next, I rub my index and middle fingers over my opposite palm while envisioning my book—a tome with a pearlescent leather cover and my life's story written on the pages, up to the very moment I access it, updated by the Angels themselves. I also receive an occasional message from the Angels in it, written in their runes that require interpretation, sometimes imperfect and therefore confusing. Thank the Angels Mom and Rina usually deliver the messages, although they can oftentimes be just as cryptic. When the Sacred Archives fell, I had eventually learned how to access my book as though it magically resided inside my palm. It isn't coming forth now, though. Like them, it remains elusive.

"Come on," I plead as I rub harder. "I need to know if that was a real message or my own fears getting to me."

Still, the book doesn't show itself. No matter how hard I rub or how much I beg. *Shit. Something's not right.* If I didn't believe it before, I feel it in my bones now.

"*Tristan,*" I mentally call out as I return to the top of the cliff. I sense his mind signature straight west, among the rubble of the Amadis mansion, exploring while he waits for me. "*I think we have a problem.*"

He instantly appears by my side. His hazel eyes darken and his brows pull together when he sees my expression.

"What is it?"

I swallow. "Um, could be nothing. Or could be . . ." I sigh. "I don't know."

I suddenly can't voice what I'd experienced, because it all seems unreal. *What the hell could that have meant, anyway? What's coming? What could be so bad for Mom to behave so strangely? We've already fought Demons, Hell, and even Satan himself. And what realms, as in more than one? The Otherworld? Could Heaven and Hell even fall? Or is there another realm besides Earth? What does that even mean? Then there's the whole Heaven's Gates closing thing, which can't possibly happen. Right? Can Heaven really shut its Gates?*

No, I decide. That would mean . . . I can't accept what that would mean. I can probably deal with the fact that the Angels broke their promise that I would never be without them, but I can't fathom the thought that human souls would be blocked from entering Heaven.

Impossible. That had to be my imagination. A manifestation of my worries about everything going on. As for not being able to reach Mom or my book, well, that's nothing new, really.

"Never mind," I finally say to Tristan, giving him a smile to show that everything is okay after all.

He eyes me for a moment as though not buying my about-face, but then slips his arm around my waist. "Ready to go home, then? Or . . ."

He leans his head down to brush his lips over mine.

I return the kiss, but only briefly. "As much as I like that *or*, our daughters are waiting for us."

"I doubt it. You'd been meditating for a while. They're probably done training by now and foraging for Blossom."

I glance up at the sky, realizing for the first time how far the sun had already moved. "All the more reason to get home sooner. We can continue that *or* tonight."

Giving him another smile, I lift on my toes to kiss him one more time.

Then I mentally call out for the rest of my core council. Just before we pass through the magical portal that will take us back to The Loft, we all notice the darkening of the sky.

I look up over my shoulder, surprised to find what I hadn't seen only moments ago. "Huh. That's weird. Looks like a solar eclipse. Was I told about this and don't remember?"

Tristan shakes his head. "No. The record keepers didn't say anything about it. They might need an audit on their calendars."

That's one of many problems with the entire world being destroyed and then all of life existing underground for five years during the worst of the fallout—a loss of continuity of the world's clocks and calendars. Experts around the world have done their best to reset everything as close as possible to what they think would be right, and they recalibrate them every year. By now, we know moon and star cycles, but the accuracy of predicting events such as eclipses is apparently lacking. Of course, the black magic causes all kinds of weirdness and exacerbates the problem, especially when it's stirred up by all of the crazy weather and natural disasters.

I gnaw on my bottom lip for a moment as I consider this. "Yeah. We need to make sure that gets done."

Glancing up at the darkening sky one more time before passing through the portal, I hope that's all it is—a miscalculation of their calendars—but knowing just as well as Tristan surely does that the explanation isn't right. First a warning about the girls that may or may not have come from my Angelic mother and grandmother, followed by the possibility of Heaven's Gates closing. And now this. Chalking it all up to coincidence and miscalculations just doesn't sit right in my gut—but oh, how I want to believe that.

CHAPTER 7

*W*hen we step through the portal, passing from what once had been the Greek Isles to the middle of the North American continent, the sun remains obliterated.

"I'm pretty sure that's not an eclipse," Owen says as we stride through the woods near The Loft. Because of the boundary wards, we can't portal or flash directly to the entrance.

"Not when we just traveled halfway around the world in two seconds, and the same phenomenon is happening here at the same time," Tristan agrees, his eyes scanning the sky through the tree limbs.

"At least our record keepers aren't off with the calendars," I say. "But if it's not an eclipse, what the hell is it? Another black magic effect?"

"That would be my guess," Owen says. "It definitely feels dark."

"I don't like it," Tristan murmurs from my side.

"I don't either," I reply quietly, thinking about what happened on Amadis Island. Well, not *on* the island—I'd physically been on the island, but had I spiritually been at Heaven's Gates again? Is that related to this? Perhaps Tristan can help me work through it and probably help me see that I'm blowing the vision out of proportion, that it's all in my head and nothing more. That this odd shit in the sky is totally unrelated and just another weather phenomenon that will eventually blow away.

"Mom! Dad!" The girl's panic-filled screech makes my heart stutter for a moment before my brain registers that the scream hadn't been for us. Charleigh, with orange hair flying like a flame behind her, sprints toward us and her parents just behind us. But when her gaze falls on me and flies to Tristan, she stops dead in her tracks, and her flame-colored eyes widen.

"Charleigh, what's wrong?" I ask, reaching for her, but Blossom is suddenly at her daughter's side.

"What's going on, sweetie?" she asks, sliding her arm around Charleigh's shoulders.

The teen's gaze bounces between her mother and me, and I can see fear growing in them with each heartbeat. Her throat bobs with a swallow before she finally speaks. "It's ... it's the twins. Something's wrong." She blinks against the tears brimming. "I'm sorry, Aunt Alexis. I got here as fast as I could, but the wards wouldn't let me flash all the way here, which you know, of course, and then I finally made it but you weren't here yet, so I went back and—"

"What's wrong with the twins?" Tristan asks, cutting off her babble, a trait she'd learned from her mother. Charleigh only does it when she's nervous or scared, though.

"They ... they weren't there. It's like they disappeared into thin air. I don't know what happened to them!"

I feel like I've been punched in the gut, the air whooshing out of me.

"What about Sasha?" I manage to ask, clinging on to a thread of hope.

Charleigh shakes her head. "I don't know. She's gone, too. Maybe she's with them?"

"Where did you last see them, honey?" Blossom asks, her voice slow and soothing. I understand she wants to calm her daughter down, but mine are apparently missing!

I don't need for Charleigh to answer out loud. Either she's let her mind shield down on purpose for me, or she's failed to keep it up in her emotional estate. I see in her mind exactly where they'd been—a clearing in the woods that seems vaguely familiar.

"Take us there," I order, the words a near growl.

"North," Charleigh says at the same time. She sucks her bottom lip between her teeth, gnawing on it.

"How far north?" Tristan asks, a steely edge to his tone that he usually avoids using with the girls. Charleigh seems to suddenly be at a loss of words, but I already have an idea. I glean enough to know they'd been far beyond the wards, even after their pinky swears last night. Beyond the shields that keep out the zombies and the Demons and other unwanted visitors. And then up north …

"Oh, shit," I whisper as I recall the last time our girls went missing and had gone north. I know why the clearing seems familiar. "Tristan! We have to go!"

"Show us, Charleigh," Blossom says, squeezing her daughter's shoulder. She must have realized the same thing.

Shaking his head, Tristan snaps his wings out. "It'll take too long, and it could be dangerous. We know where to go. Charleigh, stay here with your parents. Vanessa and Owen, meet us there."

I telepathically share the location with Owen and Vanessa as I follow Tristan's lead, revealing my wings and launching into the sky with him. They'll have to run beyond the wards before they can flash, and we don't have time for that. Not if it's true—that the girls found or somehow reopened that same strange portal they had ten years ago.

But how? Owen had sealed it shut and cloaked it so well, none of us had been able to find it again. We thought it had disappeared completely, and it had been so long now, we'd almost forgotten all about it. But as I fly north, I recall the dark energy that had oozed out of it before—the same kind of energy we all feel now. And I can't help but wonder if that portal has been the cause of the darkness spreading around the world all this time.

Is it the cause of the "eclipse," too?

Summer had finally come a couple of weeks ago, and there's already some new growth among the trees, though most remain bare. The normal trees, anyway. A bright fuchsia-colored one swings its tallest branches toward me as I pass high over it, steering clear of the flesh-eating tree's reach. A dozen or so beheaded zombies, dead for good, are piled near it, and I wonder if the girls had done that or someone else. I don't panic about any of these threats—the girls aren't six anymore. They're very well trained and can hold their own.

It's the portal that scares the shit out of me.

Not too far past the tree and pile of corpses, we come to the spot where the twins had been found by Owen and Vanessa so many years ago. Even if we hadn't known where to go, the clearing would have definitely caught our attention, from the ground or the air. For another new kind of foliage seems to be growing there—a dark, undulating mass from the sky becomes a tangled mess of black, thorny vines and branches encircling one edge of the clearing. That same dark energy permeates through the overgrowth.

"None of this was in Charleigh's mind when she envisioned the clearing," I say as Tristan and I reach the ground. "It's grown this much already?"

"What is it?" Vanessa asks, flying through the trees on the far side of the clearing.

She stops next to Tristan and me as we study it for a moment. Even as we watch, ebony tendrils grow and entwine with others, adding a few inches to the mass in seconds.

"You don't think the girls are in there, do you, Tristan?" I don't sense them, not their mind signatures or their energy. Although ... I can sense a trace of their energies. And somebody else's ... "Dorian's been here," I whisper, my heart skipping a beat.

Owen finally appears next to Vanessa, and without a word to us, he mutters a chant under his breath as he flicks his fingers in the air. What looks like dust particles catch the light, glowing in muted colors as they linger in the space around us, scattered and faint.

"The lighter brown is Brielle's energy," Owen says. "The bluish-gray is Elliana's. And the dark gray—" He looks at me and frowns, confirming what I'd said right before he flashed in to join us. "Dorian."

"What about Sasha's energy?" I ask.

Owen points to a few flecks of a very faint lavender color. "She was here, but I don't know if she's with them."

Tristan rubs his jaw and stubble-covered chin. "I don't think the girls are trapped in these vines. I do think the portal's in there."

My heart takes another tumble. "You don't think Dorian did this, do you? Took them through the portal?"

I shake my head, denying my own theory. No way. He wouldn't stoop this low. Would he? The energy here is so dark—even darker than Dorian's. Although, admittedly, it's been so long since I've seen my son, I don't honestly know how bad he might be now. The stories ... I shake my head again. I refuse to believe the stories. I refuse to believe his own claim that he's a monster. My son has a good heart and soul—buried deeply, though it might be.

"We need to find out," I say.

"Stand back," Owen orders, although he doesn't wait for us to move before he shoots a spell at the vines directly in front of us. His magic cuts a gap into them at the same time a high-pitched shrieking pierces my eardrums—as though the vines themselves scream in agony. But within seconds of the severed parts hitting the ground, new branches grow to replace them.

I reach out to touch an onyx cord, but it shrinks away from me. When I step closer, an entire section pulls apart—whether inviting me in or afraid of my touch, I'm not sure.

"Alexis—" Owen starts as I continue forward.

"My daughters could be lost in here," I throw over my shoulder, cutting my protector off before he insists that I stay back. "Don't *Alexis* me. I'm not arguing with you about this. They can't be that far in anyway."

"Unless everything closes in on us and swallows us whole."

It's not an entirely irrational theory. Not with the new kinds of vegetation that are more like monsters than plants, including those like the fuchsia one that like the taste of human flesh.

Deciding to test this one, I step forward again, partially in the arch of the black vines, and lift my arms to my sides, stretching my fingers out in both directions. The entanglement pulls farther away, widening the space. "I don't think it will. I think it's . . . afraid of me. Maybe all of us."

Vanessa comes up next to me and barely touches one of the branches with a finger. It doesn't pull away. Instead there's a sizzling sound, and Vanessa jerks her hand back. Smoke rises from the damaged branch as well as from the tip of her finger.

"Definitely black magic," she says, shaking her hand as though the touch actually hurt her vampire flesh.

Tristan walks up to my other side, and the vines pull back even farther. "Which would explain why you and Owen can damage it, but Alexis is right—it actually seems to fear her and me."

"See? Tristan and I *have* to go." My tone doesn't give room for argument. Not when my gut tells me my girls are through these vines.

Owen blows out a sigh of resignation.

"Nothing ventured, nothing gained," Vanessa mutters, but she hesitates rather than stepping closer to us as she eyes the closest thorny branch. "You two go first. Open it up."

"You're a damn vampire. It doesn't seriously hurt you, does it?" My patience is waning, making my tone curt.

"It doesn't tickle. Not as bad as your electric shock, but I remember all too well what my beautiful porcelain skin looked like after you fried me. Black and wrinkly and ugly!"

"So the vine shocked you?"

She pulls a face. "Not exactly the same. It's like a shock of the worst kind of evil, jolting through your veins and right into your soul." Her shoulders tremble as a shudder racks through her. I'm reminded of the sensation when I touched Dorian all those years ago and frown. "Like the Amadis power you gave me before I converted, but . . . the opposite. And so much worse."

"All from that one little touch?"

"Exactly. Which is why I'd prefer not to do so again, especially with my whole body."

"Fair enough." I turn and walk ahead with Tristan at my side, and the vines continue to shrink far away from us.

We're all within the outside border when Owen yelps. "Dudes!"

We both turn to see the opening closing up behind us. Maybe it really will swallow us up after all. Tristan walks back, and the branches retreat again.

"We'll have to flank them," he says to me as he stands behind Owen and holds his arms out wide.

I nod and lift my arms, leading Vanessa with Owen behind her and Tristan bringing up the rear. We make our way through a lot more than seems possible, darkness growing around us with each step—darkness as in lack of sunlight and just as much as in lack of goodness.

"How is it so damn deep?" I mutter, feeling like I'm getting farther away from my girls rather than closer to finding them.

"Maybe it's growing deeper even as we walk, and we're not really getting anywhere but thicker into this . . . soul-munching blackness," Vanessa says. Is that panic I hear in her voice? I feel the heaviness of the black magic—the evil squeezing in on me—but I also feel confident that I can beat it. Vanessa, though, one of the toughest and most fearless beings I know, is practically terrified.

I gather my Amadis power into a bubble inside me and grow it outward, beyond my own body, stretching it until it surrounds Vanessa. She lets out an audible sigh. Then Owen does, too, as I engulf him within it. Although they're both Amadis, their power apparently isn't enough to fight the intense evil surrounding us. As I turn back to keep going and wonder how much worse the evil will get, I notice the darkness we'd been in has lightened considerably. I can almost see sky above us as light filters in. The vines have retracted even more. Whatever this mass is, it's definitely afraid of me and my powers. That's a good sign. The girls haven't received their powers yet, but they're still Earth's Angels. I hope they have enough to protect them, as well.

"Finally," I growl as we break through to a small clearing, where the vines weave together to form a perfect, vertical circle about three feet off the ground and five feet in diameter. The space in the circle wavers, like a mirage rising off hot pavement, and although I can't really see into it, what lay beyond it is definitely not some strange, black, overgrown jungle that surrounds us. The girls' energy is stronger here, as though something intense has happened.

"They had to have gone through," I whisper as I continue forward.

"Wait!" Owen shouts, stopping me. "Let us go. Vanessa and I will check it out. We've explored hundreds—if not thousands—of portals. We have the experience."

"Bullshit," I say. "My daughters are on the other side."

"And we're very capable of finding them and bringing them back," Vanessa says, her normal bravado apparently returning.

"You couldn't even pass through those vines alone! And whatever's coming out of that thing—" I flick my hand at the undulating darkness within the circle— "You really think you can survive it without us?"

"Your people need you, Alexis," Owen says. "The world needs you and Tristan."

"And so do our girls!" I bark, my tone harsh enough to stop any further debate. Moving closer to the portal, I push my hand at the space, where it should pass through like a knife through air, but rather feels like I'm pressing against a rubber membrane. "What the hell?"

Owen and Tristan step up to flank me. They both try pushing their hands through, but meet resistance, as well.

I remember when we'd come upon our first portal, back before the war, and Tristan had stuck his hand through it. Although the sky had been sunny where we were, his hand came back splattered with water, as though rained on. All of Owen's portals are like that, and so are the others we've found around the world. We can easily step through them one foot at a time, essentially being in two places at once.

"So how do we go through?" I ask.

"Jump?" Vanessa answers, and I look at her. She shrugs. "That's my guess—you have to be all in if you want to go there."

"Are you all in?" I ask.

She blows out a sharp breath. "I am if my nieces could be there."

I nod. That's the right answer.

"But are they?" Owen asks. "Would they jump all-in?"

Tristan and I exchange a look.

"Elliana definitely would," I say. She's always been the adventurous type, and there isn't a dare she wouldn't take.

"And Brielle would follow," Tristan agrees.

"Or they could have been forced," Owen suggests.

I can't argue with that. I can't believe Dorian would have done so—I don't *want* to believe he would have—but someone else could have been here too. Someone unknown to us so we can't sense their energy traces. "Maybe someone came from the other side and pulled them in."

Tristan snarls at that theory, and without another word, he charges through the portal, disappearing into the shadowy light beyond.

"That's what I call all in," Owen quips just before I follow my husband into the portal of evil darkness.

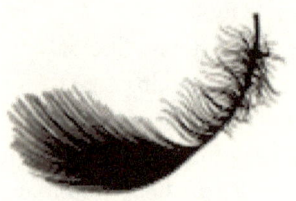

CHAPTER 8

*P*assing through the portal is what I imagine jumping through ice cream would be like—thick, barely forgiving, and freezing-ass cold. But not delicious at all. When we arrive on the other side with a thud onto hard ground, I half expect to be covered in sweet, creamy goodness, but no such luck. Vanessa's right behind me, and we both roll away and to our feet just before Owen lands right where we'd been less than a moment ago.

Dread immediately fills me, and not because of what I see—I haven't even had a chance to look around yet. Evil hangs thickly in the air here, as though the air is a mix of oxygen and malevolence. I feel like I have to fight for each breath. The physical pressure is just as strong, forcing me to lean over and brace my hands on my thighs as though a large, heavy hand pushes downward on my shoulders and back.

I draw on my inner power again, but it feels so minute compared to the blackness of this place. Focusing on it helps, though, and I manage to pull myself upright. I grab a hand each from Owen and Vanessa and feed them the little bit of power I can spare as I finally take in our surroundings.

"Where the fuck are we?" Vanessa asks.

"Am I the only one who thinks we've left our world completely?" I wonder, because this place is definitely … different.

The air is freezing, working its way into my bones, which says a lot because temperatures don't really affect me unless they're extreme. Dark, thick clouds roil overhead, letting just enough light through that it feels like dusk at home—much like the light of the eclipse that isn't an eclipse. We stand in what may have been a field or a vast plain, blanketed in a gray silt with jagged, black mountains rising to each side of us, looking like sharp, obsidian teeth. Far in the distance ahead of us are either more mountains or a city of black buildings. It's too dark and difficult to see anything but the points of peaks or roofs from here.

I twist to see behind us without letting go of Vanessa or Owen and find what looks like an altar made of onyx with a shimmering black oval of glass in the middle of it—the portal we'd just come through. Beyond the altar is a forest of what looks like black trees with matching leaves that eventually slopes up another mountain. The forest isn't a jungle of entangled vines like what we'd just left, although it may have started out that way a long time ago. As in millennia ago. Wherever we are feels ancient—way older than anything I've ever come across in the world, and we've been pretty much everywhere since the war.

"Is it the Otherworld?" Owen asks.

I glance at Tristan before answering. "It's not Hell. It's definitely not like what I saw or felt outside of Heaven's Gates. Those are the only parts of the Otherworld I know. Could it be Faery?"

Tristan shakes his head. "I don't think so. Bree took me through Faery when you and Vanessa almost died in Hades. We crossed through just long enough to get me to the other side of our world. The brief bit I saw of Faery was nothing like this."

"Okay, so maybe we're in a different part of that . . . part. The fae part of the Otherworld."

I have to pause to make sure I'm making sense. The Otherworld and Faery are still gigantic enigmas to me and the rest of us. The Angels aren't very forthcoming about all that it encompasses, and neither are the fae. In fact, both entities keep pretty much everything from us unless we absolutely need to know because the fate of the world—or at least a lot of souls—relies on it. We rarely hear from or see Bree, Tristan's mother. She always has important fae business regarding court or royalty or something like that. Time passes differently in Faery, though, so she probably doesn't even realize how long it's been since she's been back—how much of the girls' lives she's missed.

"Like Dark Faery?" Owen asks. "I remember Bree mentioning Dark Faery once, but she didn't give specifics."

"Of course she didn't," I mutter. "But it doesn't really matter, because even if it is Dark Faery, we have no idea what that means in relation to Light Faery and seeking any help from Bree or the other fae we do know. So right now, all that matters is finding the twins. I say we take to the sky to look around. Maybe you'll see something familiar, Tristan, which could help."

Vanessa tightens her grip on my hand. "You are *not* leaving us."

"Then go back through the portal."

"We're not leaving *you*," Owen says as he, too, tightens his hold on me.

We don't argue, but that leaves us with one option. Tristan and I open our wings and wrap our arms around them to carry them. The air here is so heavy, though, we can barely lift more than ten feet off the ground. My wings feel like they're flapping against gelatin, and my lungs still struggle to pull in a full breath. It feels like we've barely made any progress when Tristan stops us. We stare toward the horizon, still unable to make out whether it's a city or more mountains out there. Between there and here, however, are large, round balls speeding our way. Hundreds of them. Maybe thousands.

"What are they?" I gasp as the nefarious feeling intensifies even more. I descend to the ground with Owen, and Tristan drops Vanessa on her feet before lifting himself higher to see. I can see enough, though. About a hundred yards away, the balls stop rolling and transform into some kind of two-legged beasts with limbs as thick as an elephant's legs and heads that look like a boar's, only about five times larger. They grip antiquated yet fierce-looking weapons like spiked maces and scythes in each hand. And they all charge straight for us.

Tristan lifts his palm and shoots a ball of fire at them. Only, rather than a large orb that he usually produces, a small sphere no bigger than a golf ball lobs about ten feet away and extinguishes before it even hits the ground. He thrusts harder to shoot a stream of flame that normally resembles the strength and reach of a fireman's hose, but again, its force is diminished. More like a trickle that goes no farther than the ball had.

"I can't paralyze them, either," he says as he looks down at me and then the others.

At the same time as Owen tries to lob a spell toward the oncoming herd, which misses by a long shot, I shoot electricity out of my palm. The blue charge is barely noticeable and definitely doesn't reach a single boar-head running for us. I have a feeling my Amadis power wouldn't work against them; besides, I'm using it to keep all of us on our feet.

Tristan's eyes lock on mine. Questioning. My own question him. Neither of us have any answers. There's only one solution.

"GO!" Tristan bellows as he swoops down and grabs Vanessa again.

Snaking my arms around Owen's chest at the same time, I spring into the air. We turn and fly back toward the portal. Which looks to be miles away now. How did we get so far? It sure hadn't felt like we'd gone more than a dozen yards. As we speed toward the portal, though, it appears to stretch farther away.

"*Try to flash*," Tristan yells into my mind right before he disappears.

He and Vanessa appear closer to the portal, cutting the distance in half. Well, at least something of our magic works. I flash with Owen, and funny enough, just as we appear, it's as though the space between where we'd been and where we are now has shrunk to nothing. The stampede of boar-men close in, weapons swinging.

"Go, Alexis!" Vanessa yells, her pale arm flinging toward the portal.

"Hell, no! I'm not leaving until I know the girls aren't here!" I kick at a boar-head, knocking the blade out of his hand, then duck low to the ground as he comes toward me with his muzzle chomping, huge ass fangs slicing the air just over my head.

But instead of taking direct aim at me with fangs, fist, or limb, he simply continues over me, a thick hoof barely missing my head as he passes. In fact, all of them ignore us, charging on, and that's when I realize what they have their sights set on—the portal.

Oh, shit.

The last thing our world needs is this throng of boar-headed evil-oozing beasts invading it. I have no idea how to stop them, though, as they stampede toward the stone altar, the ground shaking under me with the sheer number. A hammer knocks into my shoulder, shoving me closer to the ground. A hoof stomps on my toes, and I'm grateful for my enchanted steel-toed boots. Since this place impedes our magic, I have no idea how well we'd be able to self-heal. And of course, Owen doesn't possess that particular ability. Not on his own, without potions and spells. If we don't move—and move *fast*—we're going to be trampled to death.

I send a vision of where I'm going to their minds before flashing away. They pop into place around me on the side of the nearby mountain, not far from where we'd been, but out of the way of the stampede. And we watch with baited breath as one by one, the boar-heads launch themselves at the portal—and bounce off it.

The portal itself, the mirror-like surface, is as solid as the stone surrounding it.

Several of those beasts smack head-first into the rock and are thrown back into their comrades before they finally realize they can't get through. A rumble of grunts and snorts travel through the group as they all stop and stare stupidly at what is now just a stone pillar and then at each other.

"Thank the Angels for that," Owen mutters.

Vanessa looks over at him with a light blonde brow raised over ice-blue eyes. "Seriously? If they can't get through, then we—"

"*Shut it!*" I hiss in their minds.

Her lips part to snap back at me, but she clamps her mouth shut when she notices what I have: hundreds of boar-men turning their attention on us. As if they just noticed the strangers in their land, their snouts lifted in the air, sniffing and snuffling. They growl and grunt again, some of them stomping at the ground.

And then they charge.

This time there's no doubt they're coming for us.

I reach behind me, unsheathing my swords from my back. I need something big and deadly for this job, and my trusty dagger gifted to me by the Angels themselves just wouldn't be enough. And we already know our powers are useless here. Tristan and Vanessa draw their weapons as well, and all three of us drop into stance. I glance over at Owen from the corner of my eye, wondering why he hasn't armed up. By the look of focus on his face, he's going to try magic anyway. I push some extra Amadis power toward him, hoping it will help.

The stampede is only yards away, the ground quaking again from their force, when Owen shouts the familiar spell, thrusting his hands forward. The boar-heads suddenly stop. Their weapons fall to their sides as their heads tilt back and forth, twisting side-to-side, peering at us with confusion. More grunts and groans issue from their thick necks and rumble in their barrel chests. Then they all turn, curl into balls, and speed away, rolling back the way they'd come.

"I managed to conjure a cloak on us," Owen pants, groaning as he doubles over.

"Thank the Angels," I murmur, re-sheathing my swords and pulling my dagger out of its holster on my hip—just in case.

"I don't know how long it will hold," he adds.

"Well, it worked when we needed it," I say.

Vanessa snickers. "Those beasts aren't very bright, are they? First, they threw themselves at that stone, then they didn't even try to find us."

"We flashed before. Maybe that's what they thought we did," I suggest.

"Nah, just dumb brutes. You could tell by the way they fought," Tristan says.

I search our surroundings, both with my eyes and my mind, ensuring we're still alone and no other threats are immediately looming.

"So now what?" Vanessa asks. "I don't smell the twins, but the stink here is so bad, it's hard to know for sure. And the portal—" She lets fly a slew of profanity. "How the hell are we ever going to get home when we do find them?"

Nobody has an answer, not even Tristan, but first thing first: we need to find our girls before we can even think about leaving.

I open my mind and search for their mind signatures, but it feels like slogging through mental pea soup. Although they're right next to me, Tristan's, Vanessa's, and Owen's are all muted, as if several miles of molten lava separate us. If someone had taken the girls, they could have been anywhere in this god-forsaken world by now, and I might not know if they're a mere hundred yards away.

"I can't find their mind signatures, but that means nothing in this place." Pushing a hand through my hair, I look up at Tristan. "Best solution?"

He glances around our surroundings, then stares in the direction of where the boar-heads had come and gone. "This area is nothing but a wasteland. Those creatures must have come from and returned to something, though. If they're the guard or army, probably back to whatever it is they protect."

"Which is where our girls could be. Are we flashing?"

He rubs his hand over the back of his neck, then nods. "But keep it short each time. We don't know what we might come up on. Only as far as we can see."

"We can't really flash far each time anyway," I say, dropping my hands to my hips.

"Yeah. We can run faster than that," Vanessa gripes.

"Yes," Tristan agrees, "but if anyone's watching, they can't see where we're going."

So we flash a few hundred yards at a time. It's tedious—and draining. But each time allows us to check our surroundings again. I reach out for mind signatures, but wherever we are is definitely a barren wasteland with no evidence of any life at all. Of course, full-blooded fae minds are blank to me, so if this is Dark Faery, I suppose there could be fae anywhere.

"Need … a minute," Vanessa pants at one point, dropping her hands to her knees as she bends over, catching her breath. She lifts her head enough to look up at me. "And maybe some blood."

She gains her ability to flash through the blood of those with the power. Usually she drinks from Owen, but she looks at me now because my blood is extra-special in many ways. She'd not only be able to continue flashing, but would be stronger and faster, too—which we might need.

So I hold my wrist out toward her.

She reaches out to grasp my arm, but then recoils as though burned. "Son of a bitch! What the hell was that?"

She lifts a white, long-fingered hand toward her cheek, where a gash has suddenly appeared, blood trickling out of it. Vampire skin is not exactly easy to pierce.

"Ouch!" Owen yelps, his hand flying to cup his bicep, where blood drips beneath his fingers.

Just the slightest breeze passes me at the same time something stings my left thigh. Flesh peeks through a slash in my enchanted fighting leathers, a red welp on my skin. If not for that minute shift in the air, I'd think it came out of nowhere, appearing on its own.

But there's something here. Something with us.

Drawing our weapons, we all drop into fighting stance and take formation. My wings appear, the feathers hardened to titanium-like strength, the edges serrated and sharp as razors. We slowly sidestep in a circle, but there's nobody around us. We each take a step outward, widening our coverage. Still nothing. No scent. No sound. Not even a trace of energy. *Maybe they've gone on?* I start to wonder.

But then Vanessa cries out.

Owen and Tristan both grunt.

Another slash stings my forehead, and this time a warm, thick wetness rolls down my temple, and I know it's not sweat.

We all lash out blindly, having no idea if we come close as the invisible attacker continues its onslaught. The scent of blood stings my nose, but it's only from all of us—three of us who can't so easily be injured. What the hell is this thing?

We continue to move, trying to track the thing, but it's faster and stealthier than a vampire, too strategic and intelligent for a Demon. Before we know it, we've put a lot of distance between ourselves, still swinging, carving, and stabbing at the dead air. Tristan and I both spin around, wings out, which can normally shred any type of creature—on our world, anyway. But if we harm the assailant, it gives no indication, unrelenting as it continues lashing at us with phantom whips.

I close my eyes, trying to focus my mind on the attacker's thoughts. It's not like my sight was doing me any good anyway. And there ... something. My body physically turns toward it, but it flies out of sight. I can sense its energy better, though, and I'm able to track it.

Nothing but blurs and smudges of movement, but I can "see" it in my mind's eye.

"*Vanessa, behind you!*" I warn telepathically, but if she even receives the message through the sludge, she's too slow to react. A tentacle-like blur lashes at her, and I open my eyes in time to see the vampire's knees buckle, thick slits slanting across her calves. "Close your eyes," I say. "You can kind of see it."

Shutting my own eyes again, I sense out for the entity, searching through the space surrounding me.

There you are, I think. It hovers near Tristan, nothing more than what looks like brush strokes of black paint against a dark canvas. It begins to take shape before streaking away into another smudge, like wind incarnate. Owen screams. My heart pounds at the thought of what just happened to him with that kind of agony, but I keep my eyes tightly shut, tracking the thing. It stops again, taking form once more, and I can feel its attention focus on me. Does it know I can see it?

The smears of black tighten and sharpen, taking a somewhat female form. She wears a cloak of smudged darkness pulled in at the waist, the edges of it streaking out like it's blowing away, as though she were a painting of smoke and mist—except the face. There is none. Just a blank, white, oval smudge and two dark slashes that might have been eyes. One of the streaks from the shoulder area begins to take shape into what I think is becoming an arm. But no, more like a tentacle that whips out at me.

Searing pain slices across my hardened wing. A freezing, white-hot burn that feels like hellfire.

I scream as my hand flies to my chest, to the scar that remains still to this day in flesh that should never scar. A scar given to me while in the depths of actual Hell while trying to save Tristan from its clutches. Hellfire is a permanent wound, even for my kind. What had she just done to my wing?

And what the fuck is she? Is she another kind of Demon? Are we in some part of Hell?

My eyes remain squeezed shut. No way am I losing track of her now, even though my wing burns with blazing agony, tugging at my shoulder muscles as it droops behind me.

She seems to keep her focus solely on me now, as well, blurring into a stain of darkness as several of those tentacles snap toward me. I swing my right sword in front of me, and the misty form disintegrates, only to reform instantaneously. I scream in blinding pain as each of her lashings strike me—

And then everything changes.

CHAPTER 9

*B*esides the immediate relief of pain in my wing, I notice the energy shift first. The air is suddenly lighter, making it easier to breathe, to think. The apparition is gone from behind my eyelids, and when I open my eyes, she's not there either. Neither are we. Not there, as in not in that dark, evil wasteland.

"Where are we?" I blink as my surroundings come into focus—and notice two new people have joined Tristan, Owen, Vanessa, and me.

A woman with silvery hair and dark brows, though her face appears to be ageless and her brown eyes bottomless, hovers her hands over my wing, sliding them through the air as though applying an invisible salve, and whatever she's doing is working. The pain vanishes, and with it my wings as I focus on the woman. She straightens and steps backward to stand next to a tall man who appears to be in his early twenties, maybe, with coppery curls, brown eyes, and full lips. They don't feel threatening—quite the opposite, actually. I open my mouth to ask who they are when I realize where we all stand.

"We're ... home?" I gasp, my gaze swinging over the island kitchen and the bordering living room, small but comfortable. Beyond it is a balcony that looks over the ocean.

Not exactly home. Not The Loft. No, this is the beach house in the Florida Keys, looking as pristine as the day Tristan had first brought me here on our honeymoon. Which was impossible, because we'd abandoned it years ago. The twins had been born here, and we'd come back a few times after for so-called vacations, but we couldn't justify using any resources to keep it up. We'd had no choice but to let it go with much of the rest of the world.

There should be mold on the walls, vegetation invading, a musky scent in the air—as there had been the last time I'd made the mistake of visiting. The backs of my eyes prickle, and I blink against the threat of tears. Dear Angels, do I miss this place. And all the memories it holds ... "But how's it so pretty?"

"Where are we really?" Tristan asks, catching on before I do, as usual. Arms crossed over his broad chest, he eyes the strange woman and young man who stand at the other end of the island from the rest of us. "And who the hell are you?"

"This place has many names," the woman says, her voice kind as is the energy she gives off. Her thin lips curl in a small smile as she glances around. "It always looks different, depending on who's here. My favorite name for it is the Space Between."

"The space between what?" Vanessa demands from my other side.

"Between everything—between time, between worlds and dimensions, realms and planes."

"We're still in the Otherworld then?" I ask.

She tilts her head side to side. "Depends on your definition of the Otherworld, but if you mean that which exists beyond the physical dimensions, then yes, we are. You were not in the Otherworld before, however. You were in the third dimension still, on a physical world." Now her mouth turns down. "One of the darkest. One you should have never been able to access. Unfortunately, what's done is done."

Questions fly from the four of us until the woman finally holds up her hands, hushing us gently but firmly, the man just watching on with a small smirk.

"Let's sit, and I'll explain what I can," she says, gesturing toward the living room.

I don't want to sit. I don't want to be here anymore. It hurts too much.

"I just want to know where my daughters are," I say. "Take me back to them. The rest can wait."

"I cannot."

"I presume you brought us here. Now take us back!"

"They're not on that world where you were."

"Then where are they? Are they home? Then take us there!"

She presses her lips together as she backs up and leans against the refrigerator since apparently nobody wants to sit. "They are where they need to be. That's all I can say."

"Are you an Angel? Because you sure do talk like them," I growl.

She smiles—actually smiles, as though she finds me amusing. I have half a mind to knock that smile right off her face. "I've been called that before. In some worlds, I'm considered that, yes. But you'll come to learn, Alexis, that your definition of Angels and Demons, Heaven and Hell will need to broaden, become more fluid."

"How do you know my name?"

"What do you mean by *some* worlds?" Owen demands at the same time. "What kind of game are you playing?"

"Let's start with this," she says, seeming to ignore both of us. "Do you remember back when the Daemoni had come out to the humans and war broke out?"

"How could we forget?" Vanessa mutters.

"You were in England at one point, and you responded to a strange anomaly near Liverpool?"

It takes me a moment, but as soon as I recall what had felt like a ripple in the veil between our world and the Otherworld, I can't believe I've ever forgotten it. At the time, civilization was in chaos, so when a group who looked quite human but supposedly were not from our world had suddenly appeared and then left, it wasn't the most urgent of our priorities. A couple of fae had taken care of them, and we'd gone back to fighting to keep norms safe—and to protecting our own hides, since we'd been deemed enemies of the public. But that had been the day we'd learned there is much more out there than the world we know, or even the Otherworld we don't know.

How does this woman know about that, though? She *must* be an Angel.

"The Phoenix Guardians, they called themselves, right?" I say. "From a different Earth in another dimension?"

The woman nods. "Yes, you met Leni, Brock, Bex, and Hayden. They are guardians of the gates on their Earth, the one I watch over closely. Gates that your world—your whole dimension—didn't have until recently."

"Until those guardians opened it?" Tristan asks.

She shakes her head. "They didn't open a gate. They slipped between dimensions from the Space Between. No, your world didn't have any gates until your children opened them. Since only certain kinds of beings can open such gates, you can bet it grabbed our attention."

"And who are you?" Tristan asks once again.

"I mostly go by Hope, and this is Aithan. You can thank him for us even being in your dimension to help you out. He knows your girls from another time and place, and he'd come snooping around, trying to prevent something he's not allowed to prevent. I caught him and am trying to teach him the responsibilities of being a Traveler—such as not interfering." She eyes the guy sharply. He only grins back at her, a dimple popping in his cheek.

"A Traveler?" I ask.

She nods. "That's one of the names given to us. Ascended masters, transcenders of the Ninth Dimension—although Eighth would be more accurate—Librarians, Keepers of the Gardens—we're called many things. You see, all souls in their truest forms can cross dimensions, time, and space but once they choose to take a physical life in a physical world during a specific timeframe, they are there, in that third dimension, for that time. Souls like mine and Aithan's, however, can go anywhere and anytime we want, taking physical form at will. I can do it because I'm an ancient soul who's risen through the ranks. Aithan because he's a descendent of Aion, god of unbound time, who oversees us all."

"She won't admit it, but our souls are related through Aion," Aithan pipes up, his voice deep and smooth as he playfully knocks his elbow against Hope's shoulder.

"Very distantly related," she quips, though I can hear the tease in her tone. "We can go anywhere and to any time we want," she continues to us, "but our number one rule is that we cannot interfere in the physical worlds unless absolutely necessary."

"Yep, sounds like the Angels," I gripe.

"Yes, most Angels across the dimensions and realms have that same directive. Your Angels have not been forthcoming with you. Neither have your Demons." She eyes Tristan and then Vanessa as she says this, as if she knows their backgrounds. "The ones you call the Ancients aren't all that ancient in comparison to the multiverse, and neither are your Angels. Some of their counterparts spread across the dimensions are much older and wiser. Yours don't know everything, but they also haven't shared all that they do. Whether on purpose or not, I cannot say. But there are some things you do need to know. Some things that are absolutely necessary for us to disclose now that gates have been opened from your world to others. Especially to that dark one."

"Just tell us where our daughters are," Tristan growls, that steely edge to his voice that could make a Demon tremble. Hope doesn't flinch, but I swear Aithan leans back ever so slightly.

"Again, they are where they need to be—and unreachable even by us."

"What does that even mean?" I demand.

"As I said, there are only certain types of beings who can cross the veils between worlds. Fae are one type, as are Angels, which makes sense, considering. Certain deities can, too." Her gaze flicks sideways to Aithan. "But physical beings generally cannot travel like this except through what are called gates that connect physical worlds and dimensions. These gates are scattered across the multiverse, connecting some of the physical worlds. Most are sealed shut, like the ones to your world had once been, and beings who can open them are extremely rare. Gates aren't really a good thing. You can imagine the chaos they can create if physical beings can cross from one physical dimension to another, especially those from dark worlds, which are always seeking light ones to invade. So those worlds with open gates usually have guardians, like the Phoenix that you'd met. Your world has never had these gates, and now it suddenly has two."

"Two?" Vanessa asks.

Aithan nods. "The one the twins opened and the one their brother did."

"So that portal that took us from our world to that dark place was a gate across dimensions?" I ask.

"Yes. And now that it's open …" Hope frowns, her eyes darkening.

"Is that what's causing the changes in our world?" I wonder. "With the Demons and the humans?"

Vanessa sucks in a breath. "The dark energy that seems to be taking over our world—it's coming through the gate from that other place?"

Hope nods. "That's exactly what I'm trying to explain."

"But the gate's been closed and cloaked until today," Owen says.

"Has it?" Aithan challenges, and Owen scowls.

"It has to be more than closed to keep the energy from seeping in," Hope says, diffusing tempers before Owen takes it as a personal affront of his abilities. "It must be sealed tightly. Aithan and I can use our own powers to cork it for now, but it won't be permanent. It will eventually pop from the pressure. Your girls opened the gate. They will have to learn how to seal it permanently, but that will come in time. Much will have to happen between now and then."

"And Dorian opened a gate, too?" My mind is reeling with a million thoughts. My girls opened this gate years ago, when they were little. How had such sweet, innocent young children opened a connection to a world so dark and overcome by evil? And if that's the one they'd opened, how awful is the one Dorian had? "How can they even do this?"

"They are fae. They are Angels. They are Demons."

"So is Tristan. So am I, except for the fae part."

Hope sighs, that frown never leaving her face. "They are also Throne-marked."

"Say what?" I almost flinch at her tone, the spaces between her words filled with warning. "What the hell does that mean?"

"The Thrones are the leaders of all darkness. You've met one, in your Hell."

My brows pinch together. "I've met one ... Satan?" She nods. "And he's ... just one."

I suddenly find it hard to breathe.

"One of thirteen. The youngest, weakest one, actually."

And now I think I might puke. How could that be possible? She's right. I have a lot to learn—and accept. Everything I thought I knew has been wrong. If she's telling us the truth. Which I honestly believe she is. More than the Angels ever have, it seems.

"He was the one who marked your twins," Aithan adds.

"What the fuck does that mean?" Tristan bellows as he leans forward, every muscle in him tensed as though ready to attack. The anger coursing through him comes off in palpable waves, but I'm probably the only one who senses what lies underneath: fear. The fear any parent would have at such news. Fear not unlike what we'd carried for so long for Dorian and his soul. Now our daughters are just as much at risk? Or more?

"During the war, when you followed Lucas and Dorian into Hell—you know what happened there," Hope says.

I close my eyes. I'd been pregnant with the twins. I'd nearly been killed and them too—for Satan. For a Throne, apparently.

"When you were there, Satan used Lucas to mark the girls while they were still in the womb. Marked them for all the Thrones. All three of your children's blood calls to them, to all thirteen of them, but especially your girls' blood—their power. Dorian was marked, as well, but maybe because the girls were still in the womb, or maybe because they're twins, their connection is stronger. That link must have given your daughters the power to open the gate to a dark world. Fortunately, the Thrones aren't aware of it yet, but darkness threatens your world more than ever now. And because yours is tied so closely to Faery, it threatens that realm, as well. All of the Faery realms, since they're all interconnected. Unfortunately, since you've traveled through the gate, you caught the attention of one of the Thrones' seekers."

"That wraith-like thing we couldn't actually see? She wasn't a Demon?" I ask.

Hope steps forward and leans her arms on the counter. "Like I said, you'll need to broaden your definitions. Seekers were created by the Thrones, like your Demons were created by Satan. They specifically seek out openings to worlds that are still light or neutral, that have not been overtaken yet by darkness. It won't be long until the Thrones find out. And then..."

"And then we're all fucked," Vanessa breathes.

"Pretty much," Aithan says. "Except for Brielle and Elliana—"

Hope flicks her hand, and Aithan's mouth moves soundlessly before his lips press together. She'd literally shut him up. Neat trick. I'm a little jealous that I can't do that, but I'd probably abuse the power on a daily, if not hourly, basis.

"Brielle, Elliana, and Dorian can change everything—for the good or bad, that's up to them. They have free will, and we will not do or say anything to affect that." Her tone is firm, unrelenting, and I can't decide if she's explaining this to us or drilling it into Aithan's head. Probably both. "The one thing you have working in your favor, once you return to your own world, is time. It moves differently across dimensions—they are not exactly in synch. So you can prepare before the Thrones come. Just beware that others are preparing, too."

I open my mouth to ask what that means, but Owen speaks first.

"What about the gate Dorian opened? Is he guarding it, or did you already seal it, or what? Why all this talk only about this gate and not his?" he asks. "Don't we have two to worry about?"

As a powerful warlock, my third in command, and our own portal expert, he's probably taking this responsibility on himself.

"The gate Dorian opened goes to another Earth that remains neutral. It is not a threat. In fact, it's your world that's a threat to theirs, especially if the darkness penetrates yours—guess where it will go next. You see how these gates are such a problem?" Hope's gaze falls over each of us, including Aithan, to ensure we understand.

"Okay, so we seal them both shut, and we guard them," I say with a shrug. "This is the Age of Angels. I lead Earth's Angels, and we will do everything necessary to protect our world and all of its beings, especially humanity."

Hope leans over further, closer to me. Her gaze zeroes in on mine, penetrating as if to drive her message home with her eyes as much as her mouth. "You cannot be arrogant, Alexis! Do not think for one moment that you have the upper hand here. This evil that's coming—the Thrones and all that follow them—it wants, *needs* to devour your world and all of the souls on it. That's how it survives. It feeds on the energy of souls. That world you'd gone into? It was overtaken by the Thrones and their evil, the souls destroyed, the world left to die. They want to do the same to yours!"

My breath catches, but Hope continues, her tone becoming more fervent, as well as the look in her dark eyes.

"But more than anything," she says, "it wants your children. Beings with such power as your children's can give them access to every world in every dimension. And it's not just the Thrones who want them. Your girls are in grave danger from factions in your world and across Faery. There are some who will want to use them for the great power they wield. And there are others who will want to kill them so they can never wield that power against them or anyone else. For that power can be as dark as the world you just left, if the girls let it become so. The darkness already has its hooks in your son, and it's tasted your daughters. It won't stop until it has them all."

Tristan and I exchange a look, and I swear I see a shadow of those flames that used to dance in his eyes.

"The fuck if I'll let that happen," he snarls.

CHAPTER 10

$\mathcal{M}$y gaze traces the crack in the granite countertop while processing this news. "Mom and Rina knew about this," I murmur, and I look up at Hope. "They did, didn't they? They knew and wouldn't tell me."

Vanessa, Owen, and even Tristan stare at me, confused. I haven't mentioned anything about what happened while meditating on Amadis Island this afternoon. Was that really just this afternoon? It feels like eons ago.

Hope shrugs. "I cannot pretend to know what they knew or why they would or wouldn't tell you. I can tell you that your Heavenly Host is not very forthcoming. They do believe in free will, though they are quite jealous of it because they do not have it. They may or may not have shared this with your mother and grandmother, with any of your ancestors, knowing their close connection to you."

Close? It really hasn't been anymore. They've pretty much left us to do our own thing. "But they did try to warn me," I say. "And then—" My gaze jumps back to Hope. "Did Heaven's Gates really close?"

"The Heaven of your world?" She nods, and everyone in the room except Hope and Aithan suck in a sharp breath. "They are protecting their own realm. They held out as long as they could, even after the girls first opened the gate, but now your Host will take no chances, it seems. If the darkness enters *any* of the Heavens? That'd be even worse than the

Thrones getting their hands on your girls, if they can go right to the source of light."

My hand lifts to my chest, as though I can soothe my aching heart. We're cut off from the Angels and my ancestors. My mom and my grandmother. Although I didn't like not being able to reach them before, I'd believed—hoped—they were still there in their own way, watching but knowing we didn't truly need them. I'd still felt some kind of presence, if only as a wish. Now, though, this separation feels so real . . . so permanent.

"But you can help us?" Owen asks.

"We've done what we can at this point in time in your world. All we can do now is take you back to your home world and try to ensure that gate remains impenetrable from the dark souls of that other world."

"You said you would seal it," Tristan says.

"We can seal it against those lesser beings. It will not hold forever, though, especially not against the power of your girls or the Thrones."

"So what do we do?" I don't bother hiding the desperate plea in my own voice.

"You go home. You protect your girls until they're mature enough to handle their power. And at that time, you teach them and prepare them for what's to come."

"If you can go to any time and place, can't you take us back to before they opened the gate, and we can stop them from doing so?" Owen asks, and I cock my head expectantly, liking this idea.

Hope shakes her head, though. "That would be interfering, changing timelines and removing the free will of too many beings. It would cause chaos. What's done is done. You all must make your choices as you move forward."

The look she gives Aithan as she says this makes me wonder if that had been his plan before she found him—to somehow prevent the twins from opening the gate in the first place. I study him, wondering how he would know my girls in the future, memorizing his features so I would recognize him when they meet. While I want my girls to know true love like what Tristan and I have, it's the ones that would come before now and then that worry me. At least when this Aithan comes into their lives —Brielle's, I would assume—I'd know that he's a good one. That he'd risked everything to try to protect them.

"We must get you back now," Hope says, straightening. "Too much time has passed already. We've probably done and said more than we should have."

"Wait. Don't take us home, please," I practically beg. "Take us to our girls. I can't go home if they aren't there. I have to *know* they're safe."

She sighs. "I'm sorry, Alexis, but not even I can go where they are. You won't have to wait long. Just know that their time in your world is not over. Not even close. Their lives won't be easy. In fact, they will be challenged like nobody in your dimension ever has been. They must decide how to meet those challenges. The best thing you can give them is your light and your love. As long as they know they have that, they just might pull themselves—and the rest of the multiverse—through this."

She looks at Aithan and nods, and the next thing I know, the beach house surroundings disappear to be replaced by the Memorial Garden near The Loft. Hope and Aithan are nowhere to be seen.

My gaze immediately turns to the oak tree and Charlotte's and Heather's ornaments. Every time I come out here, I go to those two first for a few reasons, not least of which because this is where I'd last seen my son in person. When I thought I might have seen the last faint light of his soul vanish behind a wall of evil. That had been ten years ago—when the girls had opened the gate for the first time. He'd been close by that time ... and this one.

What does that mean?

"Alexis!"

I turn to find Blossom running for me, followed by a small crowd that immediately surrounds us, voices loud as questions fly back and forth. Blossom's arms wrap around me, pulling me in for a hard hug.

"Oh, my angels, where have you been all this time?" she asks without releasing me. "We've been so worried, and the news has traveled far and wide. Things aren't good, and we didn't know what to do, where to even look for you. We've been holding up as best as we can, but the greater council—"

Knowing she could go on for another minute or two, I cut her off. "Are the girls here?"

She finally releases me, pulling back and shaking her head. "We thought you found them!"

A lump forms in my throat as I shake my head.

"Then where have you been all this time?" she repeats.

I sigh. "It's only been, what, an afternoon? And it's a long story."

She lifts a brow. "You four have been gone for nearly two months."

"What?" I blink. "Shit," I whisper, remembering what Hope had said about time passing differently across dimensions. Then the reality slams into me. "The girls have been gone that long, too?"

What feels like cracks splinter across my heart, and I don't know what's keeping it from shattering completely. Where are they? *How* are they? Wherever they are, they must be so scared. What else are they feeling since we haven't found them yet? What are they *enduring*?

"Noah's taken charge since you've been gone," Blossom says, referring to my uncle. "He and the Earth's Angels have been all over the world, searching for all of you. The Daemoni claim they had no idea where you were, and some of our people picked up chatter that Dorian had been missing, too. There were rumors that all five of you had some kind of pact or something, but then Dorian apparently returned—"

Tristan's the one to cut her off this time. "Let's call a council meeting. We need to know everything. And we need to find our daughters."

There's no trace of them. Anywhere.

Hope's—and my mom's—warning echoes in my mind … for a while. Evil wants my girls, and at first, I fear it already has them. But as we search and search, the days turning into weeks, everything they said has begun to feel … unreal. Like they can't possibly be true. Although they'd been there, too, Owen, Vanessa, and even Tristan have begun to question whether Hope and Aithan were real. They now feel like some kind of shared dream, as though that other place we'd been in had created a group hallucination before kicking us out. We've even discussed that the whole thing had been some kind of psychedelic trip the moment we stepped through the portal—the gate, that other world, the Space Between all figments of our imagination. Although we *had* lost several weeks of time, which isn't as easily dismissed. And some things ring true, like the fact that the Angels keep so much from us.

I'd known this for a long time, had come to accept it. The world I'd known before has grown bigger from my viewpoint since the war. I can't dispute that we've been deceived, perhaps for centuries or longer. Or, at the very least, not told everything, whether the Angels or my ancestors knew them or not, they'd never admit to anyway. Things like the hunters.

Not even Tristan had known about them before the war. There are also the dragons and the gargoyles and countless other creatures—entire species—that had been captured and locked in Hell, some for over a millennium, and never spoken about by the Angels, as if they'd forgotten them. And then there are those who'd been living amongst us all this time, supes who are neither Amadis nor Daemoni—at least until they picked sides in the war.

Since then, I've learned of mages whose histories could be traced back to beings other than a Daemoni sorcerer, as I'd been told were all mages' origins. Some mage clans claim to have descended from the fae and others from gods and demi-gods, which I'd thought a little far reaching, but who knows anymore? Whether Hope and Aithan are real or not, the memory about the visitors from another world—Leni and the others—is definitely real. And as Sheree said then, if we are to believe all things are possible with God, then we have to believe *all* things are possible. Who am I to question that?

We'd met many shifter groups who also have their own origin stories outside of the Daemoni, again from the fae and gods and some claiming to be cursed by mages. Stories that don't go back to a Demon merging with an animal, as we'd been told. Could it be true the Ancients have lied about creating all supernaturals? Of course, it could. They lie about everything else, don't they? But do the Angels? Do my ancestors know any of this and have kept it from every matriarch going forward? Or have the Ancients managed to keep that secret from all?

I honestly don't know whom to trust, but I do know one thing: my girls are too sweet, their hearts too big and warm to become anything but leaders of Earth's Angels. Even Elliana. Of course, they'll be extremely powerful, but they'll know the proper use of that power. We'll teach them. We will always be there for them, and they will mature into stunning creatures who will protect the innocent and the good. They are of the Angels with Amadis power running through their veins.

Throne-marked? Fuck that nonsense.

That has to have been a dream or hallucination or something.

Even the portal itself is gone. Admittedly, a thread of dark energy hangs over the area, but its disappearance only feeds our doubts. Did Hope and Aithan seal it and cloak it? Or had that never even happened? Perhaps the dark energy comes off the surrounding trees, from the lingering black magic.

But where have my daughters disappeared to? How can they have vanished without a trace if not through that portal or gate or whatever it had been? The lack of answers is slowly killing me inside, and it's taking every ounce of self-control to keep my frustration contained. I know Tristan is also on the verge of losing it, and if we both do?

The Thrones might be the least of this world's worries.

We just don't know where to unleash our anger. Nobody seems to know where my girls are—or will admit to having them. As per usual, we can't find Dorian anywhere, but we know the Daemoni would have been bragging about their catch by now if they have the girls. Ragan and her hunters still haven't returned with any information from the old woman in the bayou, and we haven't been able to locate them ourselves. I hope they're okay, but as for the Demons, they would already be using the girls however they want and also bragging about it. The fae ... well, I don't know enough about the fae to have any idea what they would be doing.

Bree certainly hasn't shown up to shed any light or offer any help. Tristan and I have had all kinds of conversations about what that could mean. It could be nothing—she'd become so caught up in Faery business that we rarely see her anymore, so it's possible she has no idea what's going on here. Or maybe she's working her own angle in Faery. He's tried to search for her, but has had no luck. Even the pixie who'd poisoned me, apologized, and eventually became an ally left for Faery several years ago and never returned. None of our usual contacts—Jessica and Lisa, Stacey and Debbie—can be found, either. We hope it's something going on in Faery and not that they've been captured again by Satan—who might be a Throne, if that whole thing is true.

Shit.

At that same moment of realization, a strange current of energy ripples through the air. I've been standing at the tree in the Memorial Garden, under Heather's and Charlotte's ornaments, lost in thought while waiting for Tristan to return from another reconnaissance scouting. I glance around, sending my senses outward, but can't determine the source of it. It feels ... westward? I'm alone out here, not even a mind signature within my range, so it hadn't been Tristan or the others returning. Silence and calm settle in the garden, and I dismiss the feeling.

"Alexis."

I spin at the familiar voice, though it's been a few years since I'd last heard it.

"Speak of the devil," I whisper as I take in the tall, lithe body, the golden eyes, which are more upturned than I'd ever seen before, the points of her ears poking through her golden hair. Bree has never fully revealed her fae form here in the Earthly realm.

"I'm not the devil, but the devils are coming," she says, rushing forward and taking my hands in hers. "The girls are back."

"What?" I gasp. "Where?" My wings snap out, my muscles coiling, ready to launch into the air.

"Be prepared, Alexis," she says, her golden eyes imploring mine. "Darkness enshrouds them."

"So I've been told," I mutter before nearly growling, "Just tell me where they are, Bree. I can't protect them from here."

"You need to understand! That darkness is infiltrating this world and Faery as we speak. It's changing everything, here and there, and all of the fae courts have noticed. Your girls are in grave danger. The fae are coming for them!"

My heart pounds with the urgency of her tone, but my frustration is mounting to nearly uncontrollable anger. "Just tell me where the hell they are!"

Her palm cups my jaw. "Please do what's necessary to protect them. I cannot. It's ultimately up to them, but you can help them right now."

I nod. "They are my daughters. Of course, I will!"

"They are *our* daughters, and we will protect them—until the end." Tristan drops to the ground next to me, tucking his wings in close to his back. "Where are they, Bree?"

She looks up at her son, seeing the determination in his eyes, the stony expression on his face. "Ravenbury. They're in Ravenbury."

"Ravenbury?" I echo, dumbfounded for a moment. Ravenbury is about fifty miles west of us, but—

"They haven't been there the whole time," she says, as though following my train of thought. "They just arrived."

We don't need to fly. Ravenbury is close enough for a single flash.

I hide my wings while sending a mental message out to my team to join us, then Tristan and I flash to the outskirts of the rural town.

"Alexis! Tristan!" Scout herself hurries to meet us on the road into town. Ravenbury's leader is a tall woman, a lot closer to Tristan's height than mine, farm-raised before the war. Even in her late fifties now, she looks like she could kick my ass, and if I didn't have my powers and combat training, she probably could. Her blue gaze lands on my face, and she nods as she takes in my questioning expression, her red curls bouncing. Then she spins on her heel, talking over her shoulder as she walks and we follow. "Yes, they're this way. They showed up out of nowhere, looking scared spitless and then they dropped, out cold, as though they hadn't an ounce of energy to spare. We took them to my house in town to let them rest while we readied a buggy to bring them to you. You really shouldn't have come—"

"You know me better than that," I say.

Scout's family's farm is just outside town, but after the locals emerged from their fallout bunker after the war, she'd become leader and moved into an empty house in town. When we reach the old shaker-style home, she jogs up the front concrete steps, and Tristan follows on her heels, but I hesitate at the bottom of the stairs.

A ripple of fear travels through me.

I don't sense evil coming out of the house, but what if everyone has been right about my daughters? The Angels and my ancestors are notorious for keeping information from me, leaving us to figure things out on our own, so who can blame me for doubting them? Besides, it had all happened in a meditative dream. And that whole ordeal with Hope … well, it was bizarre and also another possible dream. Fae could never be completely trusted, so Bree's news isn't entirely surprising. But when all three have told me the same thing? Given me the same warning? Are my girls not my girls anymore?

Surely Scout wouldn't have brought them into her home if they're any kind of threat.

I inhale a deep breath and nod when Scout and Tristan both look down at me. Then I climb the stairs to see my daughters.

They're fine. They're both fine.

They sleep in twin beds in a second bedroom upstairs. I hurry into the small space between them, my heart cracking a little when I notice their hair is no longer similar to mine in color, but a rich black. I can only hope that this stark change is the only one and the darkness doesn't run deeper. I hover my hands over each of them, sending my senses out. A tense energy gathers within them, but nothing like what I'd feared. They've been through a great ordeal, I can tell, and we'd learn about it soon enough. And somebody will pay. But for now, my girls are okay.

"*They just need some Amadis power,*" I say to Sheree when she rushes into the room. "*You can help.*"

She nods, her long legs taking her to Brielle's side in two strides. I sit on the edge of Elliana's bed, taking her hand into mine and pushing my energy into her—the energy of all that is good and light. After a few minutes, she begins to stir, then her eyes flutter open. It seems to take her a moment to focus on me, but then a ghost of a grin touches her lips.

"Mom," she says, then looks behind me. "Dad. I like girls."

"What?" I understand exactly what she's saying—it's not really news to me—but is that really the first thing out of her mouth after all this time? After all they've likely been through?

"I like girls." The smile fades, and then she passes out again.

"It's about time," Brielle murmurs, but when I look over at her, she's also asleep again.

I look up at Tristan, my own mouth spreading into a small smile—especially at the look on his face. Is he really surprised? It doesn't matter. Our girls are home. And they will be okay.

Whatever darkness might call to them, we will defeat it.

I stand and walk into his arms, boosting my own power with his love.

"They'll be okay," I whisper against his chest. "They just need our love and light. We'll stand by them, here for them through it all."

His embrace tightens around me. "Of course we will. Until the end."

Until the end.

EPILOGUE

*T*he sense of peace lasts all of two minutes.

A commotion comes from outside, and I hear Scout swear up a storm from downstairs. Tristan and I hurry down there.

"You really shouldn't have come," she says, glancing at me as she loads a gun with ammunition. "I was afraid this would happen."

"What's going on?" I ask.

"Alexis Ames Knight," calls out a deep male voice outside. It's vaguely familiar, but I can't place it, so I search for the mind signature.

"Is that Ranker?" I ask. "All the way from Misery's Edge? What's he doing here?"

"Yes, they'd been here earlier looking for you," Scout says. "Not more than an hour before your girls showed up."

Hmm ... that seems interesting. Perhaps a little too coincidental. Tristan and I exchange a look before throwing open the door and striding outside.

"You found me," I say. "What can I do for you?"

I hadn't finished my sentence when an energy is thrown around me, like an invisible rope, binding my arms against my sides. Magic sizzles all around me, the kind that leaves a sharp taste on my tongue and a burn in my nose.

"Alexis Ames Knight, you're wanted in connection to the murder of Steven Marks," Ranker says.

"What the hell?" Tristan barks, and I can tell he wants to unleash his power, but we both know that would be a mistake. Ranker hates all things supernatural, and we don't need to stir him up more than he already is. Ravenbury residents are pouring out of their homes and gathering around. Ranker is known to shoot first and ask questions later, and he hates the people of this town. And me, too, since I'd helped them drive him off when he'd tried to take over control of it. That was before he'd moved on to Misery's Edge.

"I'm sorry, what?" I say. "I think you're mistaken."

"We have an eyewitness claiming that approximately two months ago, you beheaded Steven Marks, an innocent human and unprovoked, in cold blood, in the hollows northeast of here. Do you deny the allegation?"

My heart sinks.

"That wasn't a human," Tristan snarls.

"You can defend her at trial if you'd like to represent her," Ranker says, nonplussed. "But for now, we must take her into custody." My body starts moving across the dirt on its own, as though controlled by someone else. At first, I think there's a human with new abilities, but then I pick out the mage among Ranker's group, mentally listening to her cast her spell on me. So Ranker hates supes except when he needs one. How convenient. "Alexis Ames Knight, you are hereby under arrest—"

"Is this really necessary?" I ask as I try to dig my heels in to no avail. "I can explain."

"Your immediate disappearance after the crime makes you a flight risk."

Ugh. How do I explain that?

He opens his mouth, but anything he says is drowned out by a scream from inside the house. Followed by an explosion of glass.

Scout and Sheree run out of the front door at the same time Brielle and Elliana suddenly stand in the street, between us and Ranker and his group. They hadn't been able to flash before their disappearance. Are they coming into their powers? As if in answer, their wings suddenly appear for the first time since they were babies, purple and black like mine now, spreading out from their backs as if they'd done this a thousand times. Maybe it's not their first appearance. They seem to know exactly how to use them as they lift into the air.

The wind gusts around them, whipping their black locks violently, and then begins to churn in a spiral, swirling into a tornado around them. And I know in my gut that they're doing this. Dorian can control the elements. It makes sense they can, too—now that they obviously have their powers. Moving in synch, they lift their arms above their heads and slam them down. Powerful energy blasts outward and knocks me and everyone else back. I land on my ass, staring at them in awe.

Chaos ensues.

Ranker's mage tries to fight the girls. Elliana shoves her hand toward the witch, and she drops to the ground, lifeless. I gasp. Others try to charge at them, but they take them out, too, with simple swipes of their hands. As they do, flames, ice, and powerful gusts of wind erupt from their palms, hitting innocent bystanders and the buildings nearby.

Realizing the binding on me had fallen with its creator, I jump to my feet.

"Elliana! Brielle! Stop!" I shout. They turn on me, and I don't recognize my daughters.

Darkness.

They really have been consumed by the darkness.

Their hair is not the only part of them that's black as night.

I give myself a mental jolt. *No.* I will not allow it. I lift my own hand and push Amadis power at them. They stare at me with blank expressions, an emptiness in their eyes as fire crackles in a building across the street, blasts of air shatter windows in another, and the sound of an explosion comes from somewhere in the distance, their fingers twitching and jerking. They seem completely oblivious to what's going on. They have no control over their power.

"*Tristan, paralyze them!*"

"*I'm trying.*" I can hear the strain in his mental voice. "*It's doing nothing against their power.*"

People scream in the distance as more structures ignite. Several bodies litter the street and yards—dead or alive, I don't know. The ground trembles as cracks begin to form in the dirt.

"*Brielle, that's enough!*" I yell into her mind, possibly the only way to reach her. "*Elli, stop! You don't want to do this!*"

One of Ranker's men tries to grab for Brielle's ankle, but Elli's finger twitches and he's frozen solid in a block of ice.

I gasp. They have no idea what they're doing. I have no idea how to stop them, how to calm them, except to keep pushing Amadis power into them.

A blur of dark color streaks down the street toward us, toward them.

It pauses long enough by Brielle for me to see hands grasp her head and twist. Before I can even scream, it blurs to Elliana and snaps her neck, too. My daughters—my *babies'* bodies drop in lifeless heaps on the ground.

And wearing a dark suit, his hands shoved into his pants pockets and Sasha at his feet, Dorian stands between them.

Read Age of Angels Part III: Marked.

Word of mouth is very important for any author. If you enjoyed the book, please consider leaving a review, even if it's only a sentence or two. This is one of the most important and appreciated things you can do for an author.

GLOSSARY & CAST

A reminder of who and what you've discovered so far in the Soul Savers world.

Aidan - Gargoyle shifter from Scotland.

A.K. Emerson – Alexis's famous pen name.

Alexis Ames Knight – Amadis matriarch. Married to Tristan Knight and mother of Dorian. Youngest daughter to ever go through the Ang'dora and to become matriarch. Her bio father is the leader of the Daemoni. Known abilities include telepathy, electricity, telekinesis, super strength, speed and senses, Amadis power.

Alys – Recently converted Amadis vampire.

Amadis (uh-MAH-dees) – Secret matriarchal society that serves as the Angels' army on Earth, currently led by Alexis Ames Knight. Their purpose is to defend human souls from the Daemoni and to convert Daemoni souls to Amadis. Consist of a variety of supernatural beings.

Amadis daughters – Women of the bloodline of the original creator of the Amadis. Each daughter eventually serves as the matriarch.

Amadis power – A special power of love and light gifted to the Amadis by the Angels. The Amadis daughters receive it during the Ang'dora. Other society members are granted a lower level of power upon conversion and official acceptance into the Amadis.

Ammi – Started the London cell of AK's Angels with her sister Kristen. Turned into a vampire and converted immediately by Char and Alexis.

Andrew – The Angel who fell from Heaven and fathered Cassandra and Jordan before eventually ascending (read about it in *Genesis: A Soul Savers Novella*).

Ang'dora – Literally means "gift of the Angels" (Ang = angels, dora = Greek word for gifts). An enigmatic change all Amadis daughters go through to receive their powers and supernatural abilities. Usually happens in middle age, after the daughter has experienced major milestones of life as a human, but Alexis went through it quite early. Except for Sophia, no Amadis daughter has given birth after the Ang'dora.

Angels – Spirits of Heaven who (primarily) remain in the Otherworld. Most fight in the age-old war with Demons, battling for human souls.

Armand – French vampire on Rina's council, he oversees Amadis police force and is anti-Tristan. Killed by Daemoni.

Attair – Amadis warlock from Arabia who's on Rina's council and is anti-Tristan.

Baby Cakes – Faerie who's a friend of Bree, so she's helped Tristan and Alexis. For a price, surely.

Blossom – Alexis's best friend and council member. Amadis witch from the Daytona coven.

Bree – Tristan's birth mother. Fae.

Brielle Sophia Ames Knight – Baby daughter of Alexis and Tristan, twin to Elliana, sister to Dorian. Currently an unknown creature with wings.

Brogan – Amadis vampire, turned when the Daemoni first came out to the humans during the war. After retiring from the military, he started The Prepper's Stash House, a multi-million dollar doomsday prep company, which turned out to be a really good thing for Alexis and A.K.'s Angels, who converted him to Amadis. He's much cooler than his nephew, James.

Cam - A summoned son, now an Earth's Angel

Carlie – Alexis's human classmate during her first year at college. Now a doctor in D.C.

Cassandra – Half angel, half human who started the Amadis (read her story in *Genesis: A Soul Savers Novella*).

Chandra – Amadis were-leopard and member of the matriarch's council who oversees the region of India.

Charlotte Allbright – Amadis warlock, Owen's mother, Sophia's best friend, and overall badass aunt figure to Alexis.

Cloak – A magic spell performed by mages that hides or makes invisible its subject. Often used in conjunction with a shield.

Conversion – The process of eliminating dark or light energy and replacing it with the opposite, then indoctrinating the supernatural being into the new society. The Amadis purpose is to convert Daemoni souls before they become damned, destroyed, or forever lost. However, on occasion, Amadis members will convert to the Daemoni (e.g., Ian).

Cruz – A Daemoni were-jaguar.

Daemoni (day-MAH-nee) – Satan's servants as the Demons' army on Earth, currently led by Lucas. They turn humans to harvest their souls and build their army. The Amadis try to stop them.

Debbie – Faerie in England who helps Alexis and Tristan from time to time. Cohorts with Stacey, another faerie.

Demons – Spirits from Hell, some being angels that fell from Heaven with Satan as his followers and others being his creations. They take various physical forms, including horned and winged beasts and possessors of human meat suits.

Dorian Knight – Son of Alexis and Tristan, unknown creature but currently human. Known abilities include self-healing and flying. Converting to Daemoni?

Dragons - One of the many creatures that had disappeared from this realm when they were captured by Satan and held prisoners in Hell

Earth's Angels – Newly created by the Angels, on the lowest rung of the Angel hierarchy, includes Alexis, Tristan, the Summoned sons who have converted back to Amadis, as well as their offspring. Alexis leads them.

Edmund – Summoned son and member of the Daemoni. Known abilities include flashing, super strength and speed, idiocy, and being an overall douche-canoe.

Elliana Katerina Ames Knight – Baby daughter of Alexis and Tristan, twin to Brielle, sister to Dorian. Currently an unknown creature with wings.

Ethan - Leader of the dragon clan closest to The Loft

Eris – Daemoni witch from ancient times who helped Jordan create the potion that changed everything (read about it in *Genesis: A Soul Savers Novella*).

Faeries/Fae – Little is known about the fae as they tend to stay away from human affairs, as well as those of the Amadis and Daemoni. A handful do enjoy wreaking havoc in the Earthly realm, and sometimes they may even help out. They're considered Otherworldly creatures, because their world is not exactly part of Earth. They closely guard their secrets about the Faerie realm.

Ferrer – Blacksmith mage who lives on Amadis Island.

Fertility Stone – The faerie stone Bree gave Tristan when he was a young boy, embedding it in his heart with the instructions to give it to his true mate. Only when she has possession of it can he father children. The stone also allows the holder to share their emotions so he could feel his mate's love—but also the possessor's darker emotions.

Flashing – The supernatural ability to transport to another location up to a hundred miles away (give or take) in the blink of an eye. While objects can be held or attached to the body during a flash, Tristan is the only known creature who can flash while carrying another person. While both Daemoni and Amadis can flash, it's not necessarily a natural ability for all—some creatures have to be assisted by mages.

Galina – Russian Amadis warlock and a member of the matriarch's council, she favors Tristan and Alexis.

Gargoyles - Little is known about them, as Aidan is the first to be seen in many centuries. They're somehow connected to the dragons.

Hades – Daemoni HQ, an underground city in the Taymyr Peninsula of Siberia.

Heather – Human girl, Dorian's babysitter and friend, daughter of Phil and sister to Sonya.

Hellfire – Direct from Hell, used by Demons, one of the few things that can scar, severely maim, and possibly kill Alexis and Tristan.

Hunters – Humans (or are they?) who know about the supernatural creatures and kill them.

Ian – Member of the Daemoni, converted from the Amadis. Known abilities include compensating for his minuscule junk by spilling secrets, causing problems with the Amadis, and ruining Alexis's life.

James – The boy Alexis punched in the nose when she was a teenager. Later became a hunter, and they met up again in D.C.

Jaxon – Were-croc from the Australian Outback who's become part of Alexis's team. Blossom's beau.

Jeana – Sorceress who tortured Alexis and Owen to learn Lucas and Kali's secret about the Norman soldiers. Mate of Merrick. Dead.

Jelani – Wizard from Africa who is one of the matriarch's council members.

Jessica – Faerie with a southern accent, calls Lisa her sister.

Jordan – Early leader of the Daemoni who sought power over all, inadvertently helping to create the Amadis (read his story in *Genesis: A Soul Savers Novella*).

Julia Acerbi – Vampire and Amadis matriarch's council member. She'd been one of Rina's closest advisors and friends.

Kali – Daemoni sorceress who took over Martin Allbright's body. Dead.

Katerina "Rina" Ames – Past matriarch of the Amadis. Known abilities included telepathy, super strength and speed, flashing, bonding souls, converting souls to Amadis, making ballgowns everyday attire. Ascended.

Kristen – Human girl who started the London branch of AK's Angels with her sister, Ammi.

Kuckaroo – Amadis village in Australia.

Lesley – Daemoni vampire. Companion of Sonya and Alys. Died in the war.

Lilith – Bree's daughter and Tristan's sister. Dead.

Lisa – Faerie with a southern accent, calls Jessica her sister.

Loft, The – Formerly The Prepper's Stash House, a massive underground nuclear bunker that had been the storehouse for the multimillion dollar doomsday prep and survival training company. Given to the Amadis by Brogan, the owner, after A.K. Angels arrived for shelter and converted him. Sarcastically renamed The Loft.

Lucas – Alexis's sperm donor and leader of the Daemoni. Often (but not always) uses the last name Emerson.

Lykora – An Angelic being that is extremely loyal and highly protective of its master. When in hidden form, looks like a small white dog, but when in defensive mode, can grow as large as necessary to protect, has a wolf head and body, tiger stripes on a white coat, and feathered wings.

Mages – The wide classification of supernatural beings that can wield magic, including witches/wizards, warlocks, and Sorcerers/sorceresses. These general sub-classifications are based on strength of power. Some may call themselves by other names, depending on the type of magic they use, preference, or other reasons (e.g., Shamans, Druids, etc.).

Martin Allbright – Powerful warlock, Charlotte's husband and Owen's father.

Merrick – Sorcerer who tortured Alexis and Owen to learn the secret about the stones that control the Norman soldiers. Jeana's mate. Dead.

Minh – Vietnamese witch, member of the matriarch's council, oversees the Asian region.

Molita – Daemoni born warlock converted to Amadis during the war.

Noah – Sophia's twin brother, Rina's son, a Summoned son with the Daemoni and controlled by Kali.

Norms/Normans – Normal humans.

Oliver Winston Chambers – Sophia's true love who was turned to a vampire then buried under a building in Charlotte, North Carolina, for a century. Dead again.

Ophelia – Witch who serves as head of staff at the Amadis matriarch's mansion.

Otherworld – Currently unknown but seems to refer to Heaven and Hell, as well as Faerie.

Owen Allbright – Warlock and Alexis's so-called protector. Also like a brother to her and Tristan's best friend. Known abilities include shielding, cloaking, magical bindings, flashing, and pushing everyone's limits.

Phillip Jones – Human wife beater, child abuser, and overall scum of the earth who drove an older orange Camaro. Heather and Sonya's father. Dead.

Pixies - A type of fae; small, spits pixie dust that can be toxic to those of the Earthly realm.

Portals – Magical doorways that can only be created and controlled by sorcerers/sorceresses and extremely powerful warlocks like Owen. They allow teleportation to anywhere in the world just by stepping through.

Ranker - Mayor of Misery's Edge who tried to arrest Alexis for murder.

Rene – Daemoni were-cheetah who chases Alexis down in Hades.

Safe House – Homes, lodges, and other accommodations scattered around the world where Amadis can retreat to when under attack or when going through the conversion or transformation process.

Sasha – Dorian's lykora, now loyal to the twins.

Satan – No explanation necessary.

Savio – Italian were-shark who was on Rina's council and was anti-Tristan.

Scout - Mayor of Misery's Edge.

Seth – Tristan's former name when he was Daemoni. The Daemoni still call him that.

Sheree – An Amadis were-tiger who'd been bitten and turned against her will by the Daemoni. She was Alexis's first ever conversion from Daemoni to Amadis. Now she helps with conversions of others and is a close friend to Alexis.

Shield – A magic spell performed by mages that puts a protective barrier around its subject. If the subject is not also cloaked, the subject can still be seen, so it's often used in conjunction with a cloaking spell.

Shihab – Wizard from Arabia who sat on Rina's council.

Solomon – Vampire, Katerina's partner, and Amadis council member. Known abilities include being scary AF. Dead.

Sonya – Recently turned vampire, now converted to Amadis. Heather's sister. A.K. Emerson's "biggest fan" (a/k/a stalker).

Sophia Ames (a/k/a Mom a/k/a Mimi) – Alexis's mother and Amadis daughter. Known abilities included telekinesis, summoning and manipulating water, persuading others to do as she likes, sensing the truth of a situation, super strength and speed, flashing, converting souls to Amadis. Ascended.

Sorcerers/Sorceresses – The most powerful of the mages that can boost their energy by siphoning more from the earth and everything around them. Their greed for power, narcissism, and general disdain for pretty much everyone make them loners and also not part of the Amadis.

Stacey – A faerie in England who helps Alexis and Tristan from time to time. Cohorts with Debbie.

Stefan – Warlock, council member, and Sophia's former protector. Known abilities included creating a protective shield, flashing, serving as Alexis's only father figure. Dead.

Summoned Sons – Amadis sons, twins of Amadis daughters/matriarchs, who always go to the Daemoni, as though magically summoned. Include Noah, Edmund, and Dorian.

Sundae – Alpha of the Georgia wolf pack. Trevor's mate.

Sylvie (Aunt Sylvie) – Blossom's aunt and leader of the Daytona Beach witch coven.

Teah & Teal – Human cousins who'd joined A.K.'s Angels in Florida with Heather and Sonya. Teachers at the school in The Loft.

Trevor – Amadis werewolf and leader of the main Florida wolf pack. Sundae's mate.

Tristan Knight – Former Daemoni converted to Amadis by Sophia. Matriarch's second, best friend, and husband. Dorian's dad. Sexy AF warrior. Known abilities include shooting fire from his palm, quickly determining the best solution if he knows enough of the facts, telekinesis, paralysis, instant killing power, super-duper strength and speed, brooding with guilt, giving a girl multiple Os.

Vampires – Supernatural beings that are sustained by blood. They can also feed on fear and other emotional energy. There are vampires on both the Amadis and the Daemoni sides.

Vanessa – Formerly one of the Daemoni's star vampires recently converted to Amadis. Alexis's half-sister, Victor's twin, and Lucas's daughter. Known abilities include stirring up trouble and pissing everyone off.

Veil – The magical barrier between the Earthly realm and the Otherworld. Beings in the Otherworld can often see through the Veil to the other side, but those on Earth cannot see into the Otherworld. Well, except for those with the sight, but the talent is very rare.

Victor – Vanessa's twin brother, Alexis's half-brother, Lucas's son and Daemoni vampire who's not too bright.

Warlocks – Part of the mage classification, supernatural beings who are born with the ability to wield magic and physically endowed with strength and speed, making them excellent warriors. They are not gender specific and are on both the Amadis and Daemoni sides.

Whitby Abbey – Ancient abbey on the northeastern coast of England. The place where Dorian was found, where Alexis faced off with Lucas, and where Sophia, Rina, and Winston died.

Witches/Wizards – Part of the mage classification, supernatural beings who are born with the ability to wield magic, usually using a wand as well as spells, incantations, potions, elemental energy, etc. While they can be quite powerful, their powers and physical strengths aren't as strong as Warlocks or Sorcerers. Using the term Witch or Wizard was traditionally by gender, but really is up to each individual's preference. There are Witches and Wizards on both the Amadis and Daemoni sides.

Were-creatures/animals (a/k/a Shifters) – Supernatural beings with two combined spirits—human and animal—and they can physically shift between their two forms. There is a were-creature/shifter for nearly every predatory species on Earth, and they're on both the Amadis and the Daemoni sides.

Zombies – Reanimated corpses with deadly bites. Created by mixing necromancy magic with fatal and highly contagious viruses, such as Ebola. Lucas made them as an experiment and to provide meatsuits for the Demons he planned to let loose on Earth.

ABOUT THE AUTHOR

Kristie Cook is a lifelong, award-winning writer in various genres, primarily New Adult paranormal romance and contemporary fantasy. Her internationally bestselling, award-winning Soul Savers Series includes seven books, as well as several companion novellas and short stories. Over 1.2 million Soul Savers books have been downloaded. She has also written The Book of Phoenix trilogy, a New Adult paranormal romance series. Her books have been featured in *USA Today's* HEA section, on Good Morning America, and in the Emmy's Gifting Suite.

Kristie also created, writes in, and publishes the award-winning Havenwood Falls shared world, a collaborative project with multiple series, dozens of authors, and countless stories.

Besides writing, Kristie enjoys reading, cooking, traveling, getting her hippie on, and feeding her addictions to coffee, chocolate, cheese, and her latest TV obsession. She has lived in eleven states, but currently calls Florida home.

CONNECT WITH ME ONLINE

I love to hear from and connect with readers. Please don't be shy.

Facebook Reader Group: https://www.facebook.com/groups/ClubKC.
KristieCook

Email: kristie@kristiecook.com

Author's Website & Blog: http://www.KristieCook.com

Facebook: http://www.facebook.com/AuthorKristieCook

Goodreads: https://www.goodreads.com/KristieCook

Instagram: http://instagram.com/kristiecookauth

BookBub: https://www.bookbub.com/authors/kristie-cook

Word of mouth is very important for any author. If you enjoyed the book, please consider leaving a review, even if it's only a sentence or two. This is one of the most important and appreciated things you can do for an author.

ACKNOWLEDGMENTS

Gratitude first goes to my Creator, my eternal Source of life, love, and creativity—and everything else.

Much love and appreciation to my family, near and far, by blood and by choice, living and all those who came before us. I wouldn't be here without you. Thank you for all you've done so that I can be the best me possible.

I forever grateful to Stacey Nixon, Heather Wakefield, Jessie de Schepper, Terry Frank, E.J. Fechenda, and Shantell Nelson for your feedback and eagle eyes. Without you, this book could have been quite embarrassing.

To my readers, particularly to all of those who insisted there's more to Alexis's story (you were right!), thank you, thank you, thank you. Your support means everything to me! Your love for these characters and these stories, your insatiable need to read more, your excitement and passion that inspires others to read—these are reasons I write. YOU are the reason I publish. I cannot thoroughly express how grateful I am for you, and for your patience. I hope you enjoy these new stories in the Soul Savers world as much as you loved the originals. I can't wait for you to see what's coming! Also, sorry-not-sorry about that cliffhanger.

I love you all—until the end of forever and always.

AN EXCERPT

My children are powerful. Dangerous. Deadly. And supposedly they're marked. Whatever the hell that means.

Part III: Marked

Two years ago, tragedy struck. Not once. Not twice. But three times. And we're still dealing with the aftermath. I hate the actions we had to take at the time, but I know they were necessary for the protection of everyone. And now all of our efforts, all of our caution and sacrifices might be unraveling.

We're still trying to figure out what it means to be "marked," but the truth in the warnings is becoming quite clear. The factions are delineating, alliances are being forged, and war seems imminent. Even the fae are getting involved, for their realm is at stake, too—and they seem more than willing to sacrifice ours for their own benefit.

And my children are at the center of it all.

As I continue to fight for peace and prevent another war, I'm once again facing the challenge of the past: how far I'll go to save the ones I love. This time, though, the answer might prove to be *too* far.

AGE OF ANGELS PART III: MARKED

AN EXCERPT

*M*y boots balance on the edge of the turbine's stationary blade as my wings hold me steady high above the town of Ravenbury. The townspeople go about their day, finishing up chores as the sun lowers in the western sky, casting that golden glow over the lands. Many people filter down the streets from the farms and crops on the edge of town, done with their work for the day. They aren't much—the farms and crops. The lands and the air and the waters still aren't back to normal. But Scout, the mayor, and her people have been able to protect enough of their crops and livestock to keep the town's residents from starving for this long. Hopefully, their situation will improve if we can get this turbine going and producing power again.

"Ready, Mom?" Brielle calls from below, her father by her side. She looks up at me with excited anticipation in her dark eyes, her black hair hanging down her back in a simple braid that's caught between the collar of her red flannel shirt and the tank she wears under it. The tank, her black leather pants, and boots are enchanted fighting gear. The flannel is a statement—particularly to her twin—that she couldn't care less what she wears or how she looks, a total affront to Elliana.

My gaze swings out over the town, looking for my other daughter but not seeing her, as I reply to Brielle and Tristan. "Ready!"

I fly up to the next highest blade and grasp the top edge with both hands. If not for my wings, it probably appears as though I'm hanging from the blade, my legs dangling as I wait for the word. Tristan's sandy-brown head bends closely to his daughter's dark one as they make some last-minute adjustments to the contraption they've been working on for weeks. When he looks up at me with those stunning hazel eyes, I can't help but smile. We've been together for how long now? And he still takes my breath away. Especially when he returns my smile and winks.

"Okay, Mom, do it!" Brielle yells, bouncing on the balls of her feet with excitement.

With all of my supernatural strength, I shove on the blade. It doesn't budge at first, and I think they might need to apply more lubrication to the rotor—or whatever they need to do, I confess to not understanding any of it, or really trying to understand, to be honest, because that's their thing—but then I feel a slight movement. Using my wings and all my weight as leverage, I push harder, and ever so slowly, the blades begin to move. I quickly fly out of the way, then fan the air, creating the wind to get it going.

Brielle whoops with glee from below.

Then we all watch, perfectly still with bated breath for a long, drawn-out moment, before lights flicker on one by one, illuminating windows in the falling dusk. Cheers start echoing from the residents. The town has been without power for several weeks, when a particularly bad electrical storm shut down the turbine and all of its components. With a mix of science and magic—our go-to solution anymore—Tristan, Brielle, and a small team had worked diligently to fix each piece in the chain that brings electricity to the town's homes and businesses. Until now, though, they haven't been able to get the blades themselves to turn, as though they'd been frozen or welded in place by the magical effects of that last storm. It's all more complex than I choose to give the time to figure out, so I've stayed out of most of it until now. When Brielle said this morning at breakfast that she had an idea for how to break the seal on the blades and she asked me to help, of course I couldn't say no.

This is one of the many ways my family has been making reparations to the town of Ravenbury over the last two years. Of course, only a few of us even know why—Tristan, me, and a few of my council members. Memories had been altered or even completely wiped, for the sake of keeping the peace and safety of all involved. At least, that's what I say to try to convince myself that it was the right thing to do. Guilt still sits heavily in my gut and keeps me awake at night, even when I know it was probably the best solution for the greater good.

I drop down and give my daughter a huge hug. "Congratulations, sweet girl, you did it!"

Something flickers in her eyes just briefly before her mouth stretches in a grin and those eyes light up. "We all did it. Each one of the team did their part to make this happen."

She doesn't like being called "sweet"—neither of the girls do, and not because it's embarrassing. Although they usually block me from telepathically entering their minds, I occasionally grasp tidbits that tell me they think of themselves far from sweet. Though they can't remember where they'd been in those months when they'd disappeared or what happened to them then and when they returned, they continue to harbor that thread of dark energy that is anything but sweet. They've each mentioned it to me on a few occasions—that difference they feel to everyone else, a sense of not quite belonging, an understanding that somewhere within them, buried deeply by powerful spells, slumbers a great and potentially world-destroying dark force.

To me, though, they will always be my sweet daughters. No, they're not perfect, and they're typical teenaged girls in many ways, but they aren't the monsters we'd been warned they could become. I refuse to believe my son is, either, despite his own claim and all of the evidence that continues to stack up against him. A monster doesn't go out of its way to protect anyone else, not even its family and especially not strangers in a town it knows nothing about or cares nothing for. Dorian did all of those, although his means left something to be desired.

Brielle, Tristan, and I stride down the street into the town's center to join everyone who's celebrating in the square.

"You're staying for dinner," Scout says as she falls in to step with us, her long legs more in sync with Tristan's than mine and Brielle's. She's tall, closer in height to him, and slender but strong for a human, even at her age, with reddish gray curls that bounce on her shoulders as she walks. She doesn't make it a question, and from her commanding presence, it's almost an order.

"Actually, we were just going to get the others and head back to The Loft," I say as we near the square where tables are already set up and food is being brought to fill them. While it looks like a spread worthy of a holiday feast, I know it's barely enough to feed the people of the town.

"But you're the guests of honor," Scout protests. "Especially Brielle here. Well, and Tristan gets a little credit." She winks at Brielle, who can't stop smiling.

"I just hope it lasts this time," she says, an edge of doubt in her tone.

My little engineer is bound and determined to figure out how to make electricity and magic cooperate once and for all so we can eventually bring technology back to our world. She's always been fascinated by the stories Tristan tells her about the gadgets of convenience we had in the Before time—toys, as he'd called them. Sure there are some still around, so she knows the truth in his stories, but they rarely work, and those that even turn on have little use when there's no internet or even a power grid to plug into. Every time progress is made with the power grids, a new storm whips up, some other natural disaster destroys it, or black magic fries it, setting us back again and again. It's the main reason the world seems to be stuck in a holding pattern all these years. Some claim Mother Earth doesn't want to take us back to the Before time, when humanity was virtually destroying her, but I can't imagine she likes what's here now.

No, it's not Mother Earth holding us back. It's the long-term effects of the nuclear and black magic bombs exacerbated by the blanket of dark energy that's been seeping into our world for years. In fact, although the gate the girls opened is sealed and cloaked, I swear the energy is similar as it continues to grow thicker and darker. That scares me a lot more than anything my daughters might do—but especially if it finds them, becomes them, as we'd been warned.

I shake the dismal thoughts off and return to the moment. "Even if it doesn't last, you know more now than you did a month ago. You'll be faster and better next time."

Brielle snorts. "If it was that easy, we'd be a lot further along by now. Every storm, every force that knocks it out each time is different, though, causing new problems."

"Well, eventually you'll have learned them all," Scout says, "and then nothing will stop you. I have full confidence that you will do amazing things for this world, Brielle. You and your sister both."

Once again, that gut-piercing guilt shoots through me.

Scout doesn't remember what my daughters did to her town, to her people. She should be afraid of them. She should be banning any of us from ever entering her borders again. But here she is, unaware and instead complimenting them, boosting Brielle's confidence, believing that they have a future of nothing but good. Which I so very much want to believe myself. It's probably why I shove away that guilt and the memories, so I can share Scout's optimism and belief in my girls' potential.

"While you're figuring out how to improve the world and everyone's lives, Elli will be saving it hunting Demons and other evil," I say.

Brielle gasps and looks at me with wide eyes. "You're going to let her join your elite team?"

Yeah, right. Not for at least ten more years, if I have my way. Not that Elliana isn't showing huge potential in that area. She's wanted to hunt and kill Demons since she was little. That's the one thing we know about that day they disappeared, when Charleigh finally admitted to her parents that they'd seen a Demon and Elli chased after it, the other two following her far beyond the boundaries of safety around The Loft.

"I'm sure she'll find a way to convince me one of these days," I reply, but my heart twists at the thought. While I know she'd be an excellent addition to my elite team, she's still my little girl. Unfortunately, Ragan, the human Demon hunter and leader of said team, has been begging me for more supernaturals to join her and knows there's nobody better than Elliana.

"Speaking of your sister, it looks like Elliana's made a new friend," Tristan says.

I follow his gaze to our other daughter, who's just sitting down at one of the tables with a young woman who looks around twenty or so and an elderly man I've never seen before. My jaw nearly drops open—Elliana *wants* to be a social butterfly, but she doesn't exactly give off the friendliest of vibes, especially to strangers. In fact, she can be downright intimidating. This is good, though, I think, seeing her befriend someone. This is progress.

She must have heard her father say her name, because she looks at us and waves, gesturing for us to come over.

"That's Daniela and her father Miguel," Scout says. "Vanny-Sue found them wandering in the canyon over yonder a few nights ago, starving and dehydrated, so she brought them here to rest."

Although the people of Ravenbury have no issues with the supernatural and they've been appreciative of all we've done for them in the past, everyone here is human—except for maybe Vanny-Sue. Blossom and I are sure she's a closet-witch. With silver hair that reaches her knees, Vanny-Sue is the oldest Ravenbury resident, but she's as tenacious as my Elli and full of knowledge about natural remedies and such. It's not uncommon for her to be roaming out in the wild at night, especially under a full moon. She has no fear of all that's out there, which only reinforces our belief that she has some kind of connection to magic—something she can use as a defense because her tiny, elderly frame would be zombie food in an instant.

"They've been traveling since the girl was seven years old," Scout continues. "As soon as they realized the area around them was safe, they left their shelter, coming all the way from a small town in Brazil."

I notice immediately that the newcomers are normal humans—what we call norms or Normans—which means they've been traveling on foot from that far. "Wow. Why?"

"They've been searching for someone Miguel knows."

"All this time?" Brielle asks.

"I guess it's someone special to him," Scout replies with a shrug. "He only knows a few words of English, so Dani does all the talking. She said they started with a big group, but it's dwindled over the years. Now it's just the two of them. He's such a sweet old man. I hope he finds who he's looking for before it's too late."

We go over to meet the pair and gather Elliana so we can head home, but before I know it, we're all sitting down and enjoying a meal together. Tristan, the man of many tongues, speaks easily with Miguel in Brazilian Portuguese. Picking up on a few words here and there and filling the rest in with their thoughts, I'm able to follow along. Scout's right—Miguel is a sweetheart and full of interesting and entertaining stories of the Before time and of their travels. The poor man has obviously missed good conversation with another person besides his daughter, who's probably heard these stories a hundred times—the ones she hasn't lived through herself. With each one, I'm more amazed that they've made it so far.

As Miguel talks, though, I don't miss the connection Elli has made with Daniela. They seem to be in their own world, tuning out the rest of us, to the point that Elliana jumps when Charleigh bounds up behind her. Elli is rarely caught off guard, her senses always fully in tune with everything going on around her—that's been her training ever since the girls were young but especially in the past two years.

"Elli, we still have a few more things to finish up," Charleigh says as she drops a hand on Elli's shoulder. Dani's gaze lingers on it before swinging up to the girls' best friend and cousin, by choice if not by blood. She takes in Charleigh's orange hair that flows well past her shoulders and her eyes that are such a strange brown, they're almost as orange as her hair, especially when she's angry, which she isn't now. She's curious, though, eyeing the stranger back. Dani gives a faint smile as they're introduced, but immediately turns her attention back to Elli, as though waiting to see if she'll be leaving her side. I stay out of all of their minds, granting them privacy, but wonder what kind of dynamics seem to be already forming.

"Um—" Elli looks at Dani, not even turning to see Charleigh behind her.

Brielle jumps to her feet next to me. "I can help."

Charleigh's brows pinch as she studies Elli, then she nods before looking at me. "We're almost done, Aunt Alexis. Mom says no more than another hour or so."

"Okay. We'll find you in a bit."

The girls hurry off toward the town's apothecary, leaving Elli with Dani. Blossom, Charleigh, and Elliana had been working with Vanny-Sue on restocking the apothecary's shelves with healing potions, tinctures, and herbs earlier while we'd been working on the turbine.

"Elli, don't you think you should help your aunt?" I ask her.

"Brie—"

"Brie already helped turn the power back on. Are you going to let her do your job, too?"

Elli frowns, but Dani speaks up, her accent thick but her English perfect. "I can help, too. We'll get it done faster that way."

"Sure, okay," Elli quickly agrees, standing. Her words float over her shoulder as she turns to follow her sister and best friend. "Brie is perfectly happy and capable to do it, but obviously, my mom will never let this go."

I snort as I watch them walk away, and when their arms brush against each other's a couple of times, I immediately realize what Brie already knows—there's something more than friendship sparking between Elliana and the newcomer. An inexplicable fear seizes my heart. I don't know why. I want nothing more than for my daughter to be happy, and it's not exactly easy for a queer girl to find love in our world, especially when we've had to keep her pretty isolated from other people. I can only figure it's the other girl's age—because she's not exactly a girl. She's twenty-one, three years older than Elli and with a lot more life experience, considering she's traveled across entire continents and endured many hardships my daughters have been blessed to never experience. I can't possibly know how many others Dani might have been with in the past, none or many, but I do know this is a relationship that can't last. My own heart is already cracking for the heartbreak Elli will inevitably suffer, probably sooner than later.

Trying to ignore the need to protect her by inserting myself now, I turn my attention back to Miguel and Tristan.

Tristan lays an arm over my shoulder. "He says he's very impressed by our daughters."

"Oh, really?" I ask.

Miguel's shaggy salt-and-pepper hair brushes over his shirt collar as he nods enthusiastically. His gray mustache and thick brows contrast against his deep golden skin and dark eyes, which sparkle with a heart-melting grin. "*Muito esperto.*"

"Very smart," Tristan translates.

"I can't argue with that," I say, and add, "sometimes more than what's good for them or the rest of us."

The older man laughs after Tristan translates again.

"He understands," Tristan says. "He says Dani is the same, always keeping him on his toes."

Miguel says something more.

"She's taken good care of him, though," Tristan says. "He doesn't know what he would do without her."

"I die," Miguel says, placing his closed fist against his chest. "Broken heart. She … my world."

I nod. "I understand. It's hard being a parent, isn't it? Even when they grow up?"

He laughs, crinkles spreading out from the corners of his eyes. "*Muito.*"

He continues, then Tristan translates. "He says *especially* when they grow up. They're like a piece of your heart walking around and eventually we have to let them go."

I suck in my bottom lip to bite it, driving away the threatening tears at this truth. Miguel doesn't miss a thing, reaching out to take my hand.

"*É bom,*" he says. "It good. Be okay."

I turn my hand over to squeeze his as I nod. "You're right. It's how life is supposed to be."

But not yet. I refuse to let them go yet.

Tristan and I eventually say our goodbyes to Miguel and stand to find the rest of our people.

A few minutes later, we all gather in front of the apothecary, ready to head back to The Loft.

"Wait," I say, glancing around. "Where's Elliana?"

We all turn our attention to Charleigh and Brielle. Brie just shrugs.

Charleigh finally answers, her voice smaller and quieter than usual. "We, uh, can't find her anywhere."

BOOKS BY KRISTIE COOK

SOUL SAVERS

Recommended Reading Order:

A Demon's Promise

An Angel's Purpose

Genesis: A Soul Savers Novella

Dangerous Devotion

Dark Power

Sacred Wrath

Unholy Torment

Fractured Faith

Age of Angels Part I: Awakened

Age of Angels Part II: Lost

Age of Angels Part III: Marked

Prophecy of the Wolves: (A Soul Savers Tie-In Novella)

Wonder: A Soul Savers Collection of Holiday Short Stories & Recipes

KNIGHTS OF SOULS AND SHADOWS

Knights of Souls and Shadows

HAVENWOOD FALLS

Recommended Reading Order:

Forget You Not

Lose You Not

Break Me Not

The Collector: Awakening

Savage Salvation (Sin & Silk)

Sun & Moon Academy Book One: Fall Semester

Sun & Moon Academy Book Two: Fall Semester

The Winged & the Wicked (with T.V. Hahn)

Havenwood Falls Short Story Anthology 2018

Havenwood Falls Short Story Anthology 2019

Havenwood Falls Short Story Anthology 2020

BOOK OF PHOENIX

The Space Between

The Space Beyond

The Space Within